HOT LIKE THE SUN

TERRY TYNDALE IN

HOT LIKE THE SUN

Mel Cebulash

Lerner Publications Company • Minneapolis

Manufactured in the United States of America

LIBRARY OF CONGRESS CATALOGING IN PUBLICATION DATA

Cebulash, Mel.
  Hot like the sun.

  Summary: Though he would prefer to be sought out for
other reasons, it is sixteen-year-old Terry Tyndale's
reputation for being a high school private eye that
attracts attention and trouble when Sherri McFarland
asks him to solve a mystery.
  [1. Mystery and detective stories.   2. High schools—
Fiction.   3. Schools—Fiction]   I. Title.
PZ7.C2997Ho   1986   [Fic]   85-18180
ISBN 0-8225-0729-3 (lib. bdg.)

1 2 3 4 5 6 7 8 9 10 94 93 92 91 90 89 88 87 86

For Skid Weiss — Brownsville's gift to LA

1

I was working out in my home gym when the doorbell sounded that Friday afternoon. I figured the person pushing on the bell wasn't looking for me and would go away. My friends usually knock.

About a minute later, the doorbell sounded again, but this time it didn't stop. "All right!" I yelled, stomping out of my room and heading for the front door.

I pulled open the door, and the girl leaning on the bell jumped back. It was Sherri McFarland. I'd met her on the beach at Santa Monica during the summer. I remembered that she'd told me she was going to be starting her freshman year at Glendale High. In fact, I'd been looking for her every day since school had started two weeks earlier. "Sherri," I said, "I was afraid you'd moved."

"Wow!" she answered, and her look turned from surprise to relief. "I was almost sure you wouldn't remember me."

She wasn't wearing the bikini she'd had on in Santa

Monica, but she still looked too good to forget. Just then, I remembered something else. "I was just doing some exercises," I explained, pointing at my bare upper body.

"Yeah, right," she replied, almost sounding as if she'd noticed. "I'm sorry to bother you, but a couple of my friends are in some real trouble and I thought you could help them."

I halfway wished I hadn't heard her right. I'm Terry Tyndale, and I'm a junior at Glendale High School in sunny Southern California. I've lived in Glendale all of my sixteen years and most of the time, it's sunny, smoggy, and boring. The boring part is fine with me because I'm not into trouble. But trouble always seems to find me. "What made you think I could help them?"

"I heard how you found that runaway girl on Hollywood Boulevard," she answered, "and I heard about a few other things, too."

"Don't bother going into them," I shrugged. "I guess they were about me."

"For sure," she said, displaying the great teeth I remembered from the beach that summer.

The trouble thing didn't interest me, but her smile did. "Come on in," I said. "There's no sense in standing out here."

"I knew you'd help," she said, placing a warm hand on my arm. "I'll go get my friends. They're parked around the corner."

She turned and hurried down the walk. Her jeans just fit. Well, that's as good a reason as any for ending today's workout, I thought, and hustled off to my room to find a shirt. I wished Sherri had come looking for me just because she wanted to see me again—for no reason. Maybe the trouble thing was just an excuse. It was a pleasant thought, but I knew better. Girls that looked like Sherri McFarland didn't need an excuse for seeing guys like me. Like that woman told Bogart in one of those old movies, "When I need you, I'll whistle."

By the time I got back to the front door, Sherri and her two friends were coming up the walk. One of them was a girl and if she went to Glendale High, I hadn't seen her there. She wasn't bad-looking, but she would have looked a lot better if she stopped eating for a week or so.

The other friend was a guy. I didn't know his name, but I'd seen his pink hair around the high school. He was one of a small group of punkers. Personally, I regarded all of them as a little weird, but they didn't bother me, so I didn't bother them. Pink Hair was wearing some kind of T-shirt with a decal picture of a rock group plastered on the front of it, and some military pants and boots. The outfit seemed to fit with what he and his buddies usually wore around school, but I wasn't sure that I'd seen the dark glasses before.

"Terry," Sherri said, "I want you to meet Karen Greenstead and Jimmy Thompson. They're my friends."

Karen's hand was cold, and the damp feel of it made me think she was worried about something. Despite that, she tried to smile. Jimmy didn't try, but for a skinny guy with pink hair, he didn't have a bad grip. "Come on in," I said, motioning the three of them into the living room. "Do you want a Coke or some fruit juice or something?"

"No, thanks," Karen grunted, obviously answering for all of them.

9

They huddled together on the couch, and I settled into the old rocker facing it. I bit my lip, wondering if the "real trouble" had something to do with Jimmy's pink hair. Some of the "real nice kids" at Glendale High had some weird habits of their own when it came to kindness to others.

"We do need your help," Sherri finally blurted out. "We wouldn't be bothering you if we didn't. I mean it."

I leaned forward, trying to show my interest and also hoping that she wasn't going to cry. She was close to it. "Just calm down," I said, looking into her pale blue eyes. "I can't help until I know what's wrong, so just start at the beginning."

The beginning turned out to be last year when Karen and her parents had moved out of town. They'd moved to La Crescenta which sits in the foothills north of Glendale. They'd explained to Karen that they wanted her to be in a better school and have the opportunity to make new friends. As far as Karen was concerned, Crescenta Valley High wasn't as good as Glendale, but her vote didn't count.

One thing that pleased Karen's parents was getting her away from Jimmy. They didn't like him. Jimmy had moved to Glendale about two years ago to live with his grandmother. He'd gotten into some trouble in school back in Ohio, and his father had decided it might be best for him to take the empty room at his grandmother's house. The idea of moving to Southern California was, according to Jimmy, the only good idea his father had ever had.

Not long after reaching Glendale, Jimmy had tied up with Karen and not long after that, Karen's parents had told him to find another house and another girl to hang around. Jimmy stopped hanging around, but he still managed to see Karen a few times each week. So when Karen learned about moving, she threatened to run away with Jimmy.

Karen's father sought out Jimmy, who didn't know a thing about running away. Still, Karen's father threatened that he'd have Jimmy sent back to Ohio. Jimmy laughed in his face, telling him that he wasn't wanted by anyone in Ohio, especially his father.

By this point in the story, I was beginning to wonder if it had an ending. "So you kept seeing Karen after she moved?" I asked.

"No," Jimmy replied, "I wasn't hitchhiking up to La Crescenta for no girl."

"I caused the trouble on Wednesday," Sherri volunteered.

She and Karen had stayed friends after Karen's move to La Crescenta. She didn't say so, but I could guess she was better than Jimmy at hitchhiking. Anyway, she'd run into Jimmy at school on Wednesday and learned that he had a car. Karen's parents had gone off to San Francisco for a week, so Sherri had talked Jimmy into driving up to Karen's house. Her plan was for the three of them to go on to the LA County Fair in Pomona.

Unfortunately, they'd spent too much time at the Greenstead house before leaving for the fair. Jimmy had discovered Mr. Greenstead's coin collection and Karen had boasted that many of the gold coins were worth several thousand dollars each.

Jimmy had teased Karen about the coins and their value. The teasing soon turned into an argument in which

Jimmy offered some opinions about the intelligence of Karen's father. Finally, they'd decided to take one of the coins along and show it to a coin dealer in Pasadena on their way back from the fair. Of course, Jimmy had carried the coin.

I'd heard enough. "I think I can fill in the rest of the story," I said, interrupting Sherri. "Jimmy lost the coin at the fair, and you think I can help find it."

The missing coin thing sounded like one of those little kid's mysteries I used to read in elementary school, and I really didn't think they needed me crawling around the fairgrounds with them looking for a gold coin.

Sherri pouted. "That's not it at all," she said, quickly turning to Jimmy. "You tell him the rest."

"I didn't lose the coin," Jimmy explained. "It was stolen from me."

"Who stole it?" I said, trying to keep my eyes off his hair.

"I don't know who took it," he answered sadly. "I got into a fight with a gang of guys who made some wise remarks, and one of them must have taken it."

If it hadn't been for Sherri, I might have laughed at them. They'd had a coin which was supposed to be worth several thousand dollars stolen from them, and they were sitting in my living room asking me for help. It's true I'd helped a few kids at school get out of some trouble, but I wasn't exactly a high school private eye.

It didn't take much figuring to know that they wanted to get the coin back before Mr. and Mrs. Greenstead returned from San Francisco. And I imagined notifying the police would be almost the same thing as waiting around to tell Mr. Greenstead. They did have trouble, but I wanted to tell Sherri that stolen coins weren't my thing. The pleading look on her pretty face silenced me.

Finally, with the three of them staring at me and waiting for a response, I said, "Well, do you have some idea which one of the guys took the coin?"

"No," Jimmy answered, reaching for his dark glasses and pulling them away from his face.

Right then, he had all of my attention. His left eye was as messed up as any eye I'd ever seen. I wondered how long it would be before he looked normal again. I glanced over at Sherri and saw that she'd covered her eyes. "Okay, I'll do what I can," I told them, but I didn't for a minute believe my help was going to be enough.

2

The first thing I needed to do was get the three of them out of my house before my mother came home from work. She usually keeps out of my business, but pink-haired punkers weren't my usual business. "I have to make a phone call," I told them, "and after that, we're going to Karen's house. I might as well start where you did."

I called my friend Harry Fong. He and I had planned to hang around the mall that night, but the way things looked, I was going to be busy. I briefed him on the visit from Sherri and the others. "I'm heading for La Crescenta," I said. "Want to tag along?"

"No," Harry laughed, "I think I can find all the excitement I want at the mall. And don't mind my laughing. I was just remembering the day you told me you weren't going to get involved in other kids' troubles anymore. Well, good luck, Mr. Muscles."

"Don't bother," I told him. "You'll be in on this yet."

"Yeah, I know," Harry answered. "Call me when you know why."

We hung up, and I was glad that I'd called Harry. He was a good friend and he'd helped me out a few times in the past. I knew he'd come along if the trouble got to be more than I could handle.

When the four of us reached the sidewalk, I suggested that Sherri ride with me. I figured she could direct me to Karen's house, and besides, I wanted to get to know her a little better than I could with Jimmy and Karen along. Sherri seemed pleased with the idea and quickly waved off her friends and slipped into the passenger side of my car.

I have a red Capri with four on the floor, mags, and a cassette player. The three or four guys who owned it before me kept the car in good condition, and I was trying to do the same.

"No music now," I told Sherri, right after she started thumbing her way through the cassettes in the console. "I need to know a lot more about this whole thing, so we might as well talk instead of mellowing out."

"Okay," she answered, smiling over at me, "and thanks again for helping us. I'm not going to forget it."

Her promise didn't quicken my pulse. I hadn't done a thing yet, and if I didn't find the coin, I couldn't imagine what she'd want to remember. My car wasn't that good. One thing I was sure of. She wasn't going to be seeing much of her friend Karen if the coin didn't turn up.

"Did you see the gang of guys that roughed up Jimmy?" I asked as I rolled my Capri onto the ramp marked for northbound Glendale Freeway traffic.

"Yes," she replied, looking slightly uncomfortable. "It was all sort of my fault. They had been looking for me."

They were bikers. She'd come on to one of them in the

fair parking lot. She'd probably done a little more than the smiling at him that she admitted to, but I didn't push her for the details. Whatever she'd done, she'd forgotten about it and gone off into the fair with her friends. The biker had a longer memory and about an hour later, he and his friends had almost caught up with her.

The almost part was Jimmy's misfortune. Sherri and Karen were sitting high above the fairgrounds laughing it up on the Ferris wheel, while the biker was on the ground telling Jimmy that he should go away and find himself some good cotton candy. I didn't say anything, but I quickly gathered that Jimmy hadn't been very good in arithmetic back in Ohio. He decided to go for a walk with the five bikers so that he and they could settle the matter.

Karen spotted the six of them strolling toward the stable area next to the fair's racetrack, and she and Sherri knew Jimmy was in trouble. Their screams to him were drowned out by the screams of other Ferris wheel fans, and by the time their car hit the ground, they had lost sight of Jimmy and the five bikers.

About twenty minutes later, they found Jimmy. He was just coming back to life, with the help of a pail of water tossed on him by the two stable girls who had happened upon his lifeless body. They were glad to let Sherri and Karen take over. They hadn't seen the bikers, but they knew that Jimmy had been fighting and decided to help him rather than seek help from the police.

Not much later, Jimmy was ready to find his car and go home. He found the car and as soon as the three of them were seated in it, he discovered that his money— twelve dollars—and the coin were missing. That news hurt Karen more than the sight of his battered face. She told him how stupid he had been and after that, she told Sherri a few things about coming on to bikers.

The next night while the three of them were sitting around Karen's house wondering whether they should bury all of the coins and let the whole thing seem like a house robbery, Sherri thought of me. I seemed like a better idea than a fake robbery and that, in short, was what had brought them to my door.

"Take Verdugo Road," Sherri told me, just before the Glendale Freeway was about to become the Foothill Freeway.

I eased the car down the off-ramp and up to the light on Verdugo. There I turned left into Montrose, a small town that bordered on a part of La Crescenta. "I suppose you're blaming yourself for all of this?" I said, glancing over at Sherri and wondering why she ever needed to come on to any guy.

"I am, Terry. I shouldn't have been friendly with that guy. There wasn't anything nice about him."

"Well," I said, "you can blame yourself all you want, but there are a couple of things you should think about first. One, Karen shouldn't have agreed to allow the coin to leave her house. Two, you didn't hire Jimmy to guard you. The biker was your problem, and I guess you could have handled him by yourself. Three, you're not going to be much help to me if you keep on feeling sorry for yourself."

Number three cheered her up. "Do you really think I can help you?" she asked, reaching over and holding my arm.

"Sure," I said, thinking mostly about her hand on my arm, "and the first thing you can do is tell me which way to turn on Foothill Boulevard."

As it turned out, Karen's house wasn't the best one in La Crescenta, but it was close. The pool and tennis court helped to make it a lot better than the little house I lived in. I stopped in the circular drive behind the ugly-looking Volkswagen that Jimmy was driving. He and Karen were sitting in it, waiting for us. I guessed the Greensteads were into Cadillacs and asked Sherri about that as we climbed out of the car. "Mr. Greenstead has a Mercedes, and Mrs. Greenstead has some little thing—I think it's a BMW. It must be in the garage. Karen told me that they took the Mercedes to the airport."

I didn't comment. I wasn't sure, but if I had to guess, I would have guessed that Mrs. Greenstead was one of those good old-fashioned women who were against work-ing women—even widows like my mother. It was a mean guess, but I was beginning to feel a little mean and won-dering what Sherri and Jimmy liked about Karen. She seemed awfully spoiled to me.

The inside of the house matched the richness I'd noticed outside. Karen led us into the den and once I had agreed to a cold soda, the others agreed to one, too. I sat on a small sofa next to Sherri and Jimmy dropped into another small sofa facing us. He was wearing the sunglasses again, so I didn't feel self-conscious about looking at him. "Did you get in any swings at the bikers?" I asked, almost certain that he hadn't.

"I don't even remember what hit me or who hit me," Jimmy answered. "I was walking alongside the guy I was supposed to fight, so I'm pretty sure he didn't hit me."

"He wasn't the first one to hit you," I said, correcting Jimmy, "but he probably got in a kick or two. Hands don't usually do as much damage as you've got."

"I figured I might have been kicked," Jimmy said. "I had a big lump on my head, too."

Sherri looked as if she didn't want to hear anymore, and I'd heard enough about Jimmy's beating. Besides, Karen arrived with the sodas. I quickly washed some of the dust down my throat, and the others did the same. I could tell they were waiting for me to do something, and I thought hard while I tossed down the rest of my Coke. Finally, I said, "When are your parents coming home?"

"Monday morning," Karen answered. "I think they hope to be here before I leave for school."

I had guessed Sunday, so her answer gave me almost an extra day. It wasn't much of a break, but I figured I needed every minute I could get. "How many days will it be before your father looks at his coin collection?"

Karen frowned. "He might look at it as soon as he gets home. I just don't know. He's weird about those coins. He *likes* to look at them."

"Right now, so would I. Maybe I can get some idea what I'm looking for."

We didn't have far to go. Mr. Greenstead's full collection filled only one drawer in the wall unit in the den. He kept the coins in rectangular folders, and the top one had a blank space under the clear plastic that held the coins in place. The coin spaces were numbered and on the facing top of the folder, he had printed the names of the coins on lines alongside numbers that corresponded with the spaces. If the printing was right and there seemed to be no reason to doubt it, the missing coin was an "1827 2½ D. (F)." Well, I'd learned something. The U.S. had once made 2½ dollar coins, and Mr. Greenstead had collected six of them. Now he had five.

"Would you get me a piece of paper and a pencil?" I asked Karen.

While she went for them, I tried to determine if any of the other coins looked exactly like the missing one. Sherri and Jimmy weren't sure and when Karen returned she had nothing better to offer. "What difference does it make?" she asked, as I wrote down the name of the coin and outlined its size. "The bikers will have only one old coin."

"If they still have the coin," I said, handing back the pencil. "Maybe they sold it already. Or maybe it isn't worth anything near what you think it's worth. Maybe I can buy you another one for a few dollars and save myself a lot of time."

Karen grinned appreciatively. "That's wonderful," she said. "That would be some laugh on my father if I replaced the old thing for a few dollars. What are we going to do—go to a coin store? There are a few of them in Pasadena."

"You're partly right," I answered. "I'm going to a coin store. It won't take me long, but to be honest with you, I don't think you should get your hopes up about buying another coin for a few dollars. I think the coin is going to be worth a lot and if so, the next step is going to be to try to find the bikers. So you think about them while I'm gone."

I stuffed the paper with the coin information on it into my pocket and headed for the front door. "I think you'll save some time if I go with you," Sherri called after me.

I turned and looked at her. I couldn't help thinking of a lot of good reasons for having her along, but saving time wasn't one of them. "What are you going to do," I said, "run into the store while I keep the motor running?"

"I'm going to tell you all about the bike the guy was riding," she said proudly. "I'm also going to tell you where he bought it."

I was hoping she had the facts to match her boast, but the excuse for having her along for the ride was good enough for the moment. "Come on," I said, "Karen, I'll see you and Jimmy later."

"Good luck," Karen called, as Sherri hustled across the room to catch up with me.

I waved to Karen and Jimmy, thinking that I was going to need plenty of that good luck. By my count, I had about sixty hours to find the coin and during some of those hours, I was going to have to get some sleep.

3

A few minutes later, I pulled into an Arco station on Foothill Boulevard. "I have to make a couple of phone calls," I told Sherri. "If you want to use the rest room, go ahead."

The first call didn't take long. My mother had guessed that I wasn't going to be home for dinner. I told her that I would probably be home late.

Then after consulting the yellow pages, I called Harry Fong. "I was just going to leave for the mall," Harry said. "Did you change your mind or are you in trouble already?"

"Neither," I said, "but I need your expert help. I'm heading for Pasadena to see a coin dealer. There are four of them listed in the phone book."

"Say no more," Harry interrupted. "Go to Sam's on Colorado Street. He's supposed to be the best in Pasadena."

"Okay," I said, "but tell me one more thing before I hang up. How do you know about Sam's?"

"After I talked to you, I called a kid from school who collects coins and asked him about dealers. That was, as you would say, a good guess on my part."

"Your guesses always amaze me," I told Harry. "Thanks. I'll keep you posted."

"Do that," Harry replied. "I'll be around later on."

I was glad I had a friend like Harry. I was going to tell Sherri about him, but before I had the chance, she said, "Am I keeping you from a date?"

I was a little surprised by the question and the tone of her voice. Glancing over at her, I could see a spark of anger in her blue eyes and some color in her cheeks. I laughed.

"What's so funny?" she asked.

"You," I replied. "I was just calling my mother to tell her to forget about dinner, and a friend of mine named Harry Fong to get some information about coin dealers, but if I had known that you cared, I would have told you about the calls before I made them."

Sherri stopped frowning. "I was just wondering," she said. "I'm sorry."

"Listen," I told her, "you're my date for dinner—after we see the coin dealer. We do have to eat, don't we?"

"Sure," she said, as I turned onto the 210 Freeway to Pasadena, "that'll be nice."

I didn't know what was going on in her pretty blonde head, but I turned our conversation back to her biker friend.

"His machine was a Kawasaki," Sherri reported. "It was new and decked out with a lot of chrome extras. It was really slick, so I'm sure the people at Van Nuys Kawasaki will be able to tell us the name of the guy that owns the bike. I can describe it."

"You sound as if you're into bikes," I remarked, "but how do you know it came from Van Nuys? There are a lot of Kawasaki dealers in Southern California."

"No kidding," Sherri said teasingly, "but the license plate holder with 'Van Nuys Kawasaki' printed on it was a good clue. As for bikes, my little brother's the bike freak. He's got a moped now, but as soon as he's sixteen, he'll probably get a Kawasaki or maybe even a Harley. He's twelve and bikes are the only thing he'll talk about. I guess I learned a little from him."

I asked if she had any other brothers or sisters, but she didn't. "What about you?" she inquired.

"Just me and my mother," I answered. "My father got killed in an accident when I was a baby. A drunk ran into him."

Like everybody else, she said, "I'm sorry."

I smiled at her. "Thanks, but you don't have to act sad. I was too young to even know what had happened. I'm sure it would have been nice to have a father around the house, but we're getting by. Anyway, there's nothing I can do about it."

"Hey," she said, changing the subject, "I do remember what the guy who owns the bike looks like. I'll know him if we find him."

I took the off-ramp for Colorado Street and soon turned left onto it. According to Sherri, the biker was about seventeen and that news cheered me. He wasn't old enough to do a lot of the things reserved for adults, and I was hoping that included selling rare coins.

A few blocks down the street, I spotted Sam's and wheeled the car into a parking space. The lights were on in the shop, and I figured we were lucky because the rest of the stores in the block seemed to be closed. "Do you want to come in with me?" I asked Sherri.

"No," she replied, smiling enough to prove that she had nice teeth, "I'm going to find a phone and let my family know that I have a date for dinner."

"Lock up," I said, tossing my keys to her. "I may be in there for a while."

The old man inside the store was Sam. He'd been in the rare coin business for forty years. His store was bare except for a couple of small display cases and a safe. I guessed that he hadn't gotten rich from coins, but he knew a lot about them. He told me all I would ever want to know about 2½ dollar gold coins made in the U.S.

Finally, he got around to setting a value on the gold coin Karen's father had owned. "The Red Book says $3,000," he explained, "and that would be about right if you had a buyer for the coin. A dealer wouldn't pay that much. Maybe $2,500, maybe less. A dealer has to make something, son, and some dealers have to make more than others. Some dealers can hold coins and gamble on them going way up in value. But when you're old as I am, son, you're not putting coins away for the future. Besides, I can't get around to the coin shows like I used to. I do most of my selling to my regular customers."

"Well, suppose I brought you that quarter eagle," I said. "Would you pay me in cash for it?"

The old man winked at me. "I wouldn't pay you at all," he said. "You're under the age for dealing in coins. Now you look like a nice young fellow to me, so I'm not saying I wouldn't trust you, but I couldn't take the risk. Most of the time when a kid is selling a really rare coin, the cops aren't too far behind him, if you know what I mean."

"I know what you mean," I replied, smiling at the old man. "I'm trying to find the kid with that coin, so I'm glad to hear that he isn't going to be able to sell it to a dealer."

"You didn't hear that," the old man corrected me. "I said that he wasn't going to be able to sell it to me. Some dealers would buy that kind of a coin from a second-grader and pay him off with chocolate bars, if you know what I mean."

This time, I knew what he meant and as that bad news sunk in, it must have shown on my face. "Don't let me scare you," the old man said gently. "I said some dealers—meaning very few. There are some bad apples in almost everything, young fellow. You should know that because it sounds like you're looking for one of the bad apples."

"That's true," I agreed, "and say, if he happens to show up here, could you..."

"Write down your name and number," the old man said, handing me a pen and one of his business cards. "If some young fellow shows up here with a quarter eagle, I'll let you know. Just don't expect me to try to hold him here. I'm too old to try to mess around with young fellows built like you, if you know what I mean."

I liked what he said about my build, but I didn't believe him about not trying. I was sure he'd try to stop the biker. I could tell from the way he talked about bad apples. He was one of many old people who didn't like the world the way it had become. I'd never really know if it had been better in the old days, but I'd always know that they thought it had been. "Please don't bother with him," I told the old man, handing back the card with my name and phone number on it. "Two days from now, it isn't going to make much difference and even if he walks in here tomorrow, there's no reason for you to take any chances. I wouldn't."

We talked a little more before I left. As I crossed the street to my car, I looked back and saw the lights going out in the coin store. I guessed I'd been keeping Sam from his dinner, and I'd also been keeping the pretty girl in my car from hers. I didn't feel very hungry. Thinking about bad apples had ruined my appetite.

Besides calling her home, Sherri had called Karen and Jimmy. She'd told them that she didn't think we'd get back to Karen's house that night. She said that she'd call in the morning and let Karen know what was happening.

I was glad Sherri had called. I didn't have much to report to Karen and since the gas being burned in my car was my own, I figured I could report to her when I got around to it. We were a long way from finding the coin. I was sure of that, and I didn't think Karen had the money to buy a replacement.

I started the car, thinking about running over to the Kawasaki place in Van Nuys, but going there in the morning seemed like a better idea. It was time to eat.

We decided on The Sizzler in Glendale and by the time we got there, my appetite was back. We filled up on salads, burgers, and a pitcher of root beer. Sherri offered to split the bill, but I told her that she could pay for breakfast instead. That remark put a worried look on her face. "I can't stay out all night, Terry," she said.

I couldn't help laughing at her. It was funny to think that she thought I could stay out all night. Girls seem to have some idea that boys can do anything they want, and a lot of boys have some idea that it's good for girls to think that. I'm an exception. "Neither can I," I explained.

We wasted a couple of hours in The Sizzler, talking and getting to know a little more about each other. Sherri told me that she planned to become a lawyer and had her mind set on going to USC. From listening to her, I gathered that she was doing fine in school, and I couldn't help thinking she'd be one good-looking lawyer.

She'd noticed that I worked out and liked my body. When she told me so, I turned red enough to make her laugh. "You work on your body so you'll look good," she chuckled, "and you get embarrassed when someone mentions how good you look."

"Keep telling me," I said, trying to get my real color back. "I'll get used to hearing it after a while."

I drove her home long before I should have. When I asked her for directions to her house after pulling out of The Sizzler parking lot, her disappointment showed. I realized we could cruise around for a while, but I wanted to stick to first things first. I needed some quiet time to think about the missing coin and what I had learned about it.

She lived on Chevy Chase, not far from the high school. I parked across the street from her house, cutting the engine and turned toward her. "It is kind of early," I said, not wanting her to think that the missing coin was the only reason for me to have an interest in her.

She moved closer, telling me she was glad I didn't have to go right away. An hour later, I started the engine and she headed for her front door. We'd both forgotten all about the coin and at eight the next morning, we'd be together again. We had a breakfast date, but as I rode home, I wasn't thinking about food.

4

At home, I settled into my room. My mom was out, and she'd left a note saying that she would be late. In my mind, I ran over everything I had learned about the missing coin. The whole thing seemed simple, maybe too simple.

I finally decided to look for Harry Fong. I cruised around Glendale looking for his car. At Benjie's on Brand, I spotted it in the parking lot. I parked, hoping he'd be in the restaurant by himself. He was.

"I figured you'd be here having your nightly bowl of rice pudding," I said, sliding into the booth seat opposite him. "Is it good?"

"Delicious," he said, smiling across the table at me, "but the whipped cream may not be good for your muscles."

"I'll have the rice pudding," I told the waitress, "and a glass of orange juice."

"How did you make out?" Harry asked, after the waitress had gone off.

"I found out that the coin is worth about $3,000. I also learned that it might not be easy to sell. So I guess I have some hope of finding the biker before he gets rid of the coin. And I gather you didn't meet any girls at the mall."

"You gather wrong," Harry corrected me. "I met a dark-haired beauty who thinks I'm a genius. Unfortunately, she was out with a girlfriend and didn't think it would be nice to leave her. The girlfriend wasn't a beauty, but she would have been all right for you, my musclebound friend. Anyway, the beauty and I are going to a movie at Eagle Rock tomorrow night. I imagine her girlfriend would go with you. What do you say?"

"No," I answered, "I'm probably going to be looking for the biker. If not, I think I'll be with Sherri."

Harry looked up and smiled at the waitress. She smiled back and slid a bowl of rice pudding in front of me. Then she deposited a glass of orange juice alongside the pudding. "On your check?" she asked Harry.

"Are you kidding?" he said playfully.

"Yeah," she replied, dropping a check on my side of the table.

As soon as she was gone, Harry said, "I suppose you didn't come here just for my company or the rice pudding, so why don't you tell me everything in detail. Let's set up the board."

I knew Harry was talking about a chess board. Chess is one of his favorite games. I used to play it with him when we were freshmen, but he'd gotten too good for me. Actually, I didn't think the coin problem was as complicated as a game of chess, but still I went over everything that had happened and been said since I'd found Sherri at my front door. When I'd finished, I said, "Does it sound simple to you?"

"It does," he said, "but it might not work out that way. The biker is just a piece on the board. The coin is the king. If the biker turns out to be nothing but a pawn, the king may be hard to check. Do you follow me?"

"I think so," I said, "but it sure seems as if the biker will lead me to the coin."

"That's true, Terry, but you have to remember one thing. This Jimmy checked his pockets after the beating. The coin could have been lost before then. He and your other new friends were going on rides. The coin could have fallen out of his pocket. Maybe all the biker got was cash and if Jimmy lost the coin at the fair, finding it isn't going to be simple. Any one of thousands of people could have picked it up, and you don't have the time or money for an ad in the LA Times or any other newspaper."

"You're right," I agreed. "If the biker doesn't have the coin, I'm lost. Even if he sold it, I suppose I'm lost. I don't have much time to get it back."

"If the biker doesn't have it, you're checked, but you haven't lost," Harry reminded me. "You'll just need to trace more of Jimmy's steps. You might be lucky. Luck helps, even in chess."

I knew he didn't believe that about chess, but I appreciated the thought behind it. I smiled at him and said, "I hope my luck is the biker."

"I do, too," Harry answered, studying his check, "but if not, I'll be around home most of the day tomorrow and I suppose I could even skip my date with the dark-haired beauty tomorrow night if you really need help."

"Thanks," I said. "I figured I could count on you. If you don't hear from me, I'll see you in school on Monday. I'm going home. By the way, what's the name of this dark-haired beauty?"

"Rose Gomez. She's from Eagle Rock. I think she's a junior."

My mother was home when I got there the second time. "What have you been up to?" she asked.

"Some kids asked me to help them find a rare coin they lost," I said. "I was talking the whole thing over with Harry."

"Is this another one of those little things you get mixed up in from time to time?" my mother asked.

"You got it," I said, grinning at her. "No big deal."

"Okay," she said, "but I hope you're not planning on early breakfast made by me. I want to sleep in tomorrow morning."

"I'll be gone before you get up," I answered. "I have a date for breakfast."

"Good for you," she said, "and now if you don't mind, I'm going to bed."

I didn't mind. I was tired and it was late. In a couple of minutes, I was ready for some sleep. I set the alarm next to my bed and tried to tune in on a pleasant dream. Sherri helped, but Jimmy's damaged face kept popping into view. In some ways, his pink hair was his way of looking for trouble. I'd seen a number of punkers around school being hassled by the straight kids. I'd never felt sorry for the punkers because I figured they halfway liked being hassled. It's attention, but what the bikers had done to Jimmy wasn't right. My memory of his left eye made for a restless night.

When the alarm sounded in the morning, I wasn't as tired as I should have been. I was looking forward to seeing Sherri, but more than that, I was looking forward to finding the bikers.

5

After a quick shower, I brushed my teeth and then got dressed. I usually worked out with heavy weights on Saturday mornings, but this morning I was hoping for a workout with a biker.

My little Capri started right up and I aimed it at the Shell station a few blocks from my house. The guy in the glass cage took my five dollars without saying "Have a nice day."

I guessed he'd just moved to California, as I self-served the five dollars' worth into my ten-gallon tank. When I cranked up again, the gauge read almost full, so I knew I had more than enough gas to get to Van Nuys and any other place we needed to go. My stomach growled a little, and I reminded myself that Sherri was paying for breakfast. I wasn't going to argue with her about that. The money I'd saved from working over the summer was disappearing fast and pretty soon I was going to have to find something to do after school aside from lifting weights.

I rolled down my window and headed for Sherri's house. It was warm already, and it looked like it was going to be a clear day. I could see the mountains north of Glendale, and since it was fall I didn't imagine the smog would erase them from sight. During the fall and winter, I get some natural reminders that I live in a pretty place. I don't like the spring and summer smog, but making everybody ride horses may be the only way to stop that. Like everybody else in Southern California, I wasn't interested in trading my car for a horse. Our air isn't very clean a lot of the time, but the streets are cleaner than they'd be with an army of horses parading through them every day.

About a block from Sherri's house, I started wondering if I was going to have to ring her doorbell and, perhaps, meet some of her family. It seemed too early in the morning for that kind of stuff, but I promised myself that I wouldn't hit the car horn to signal her to come out. I wouldn't answer the blare of a horn, and I didn't think Sherri should.

My concerns about doorbells and horns disappeared as soon as I stopped the car in front of Sherri's house. She was sitting on the front steps waiting for me. She looked fine. She was wearing shorts and a Glendale High T-shirt. I never thought much of high school T-shirts, but she looked wonderful in hers. She'd tied her hair back in a pony tail and in a way, she looked a little younger than she had the day before.

"Where to?" she said, as she slipped into the passenger seat and closed the car door. "I'm starving."

"How about the Pancake House on Glendale Avenue?" I suggested.

"Great," she said, leaning back in the seat and stretching slightly. "Did you have a good sleep?"

I didn't let on that she had been part of my dreams, but I did tell her of my thoughts about Jimmy's eye. I also told her about my meeting with Harry. She had to agree that the points he had made were good ones, but she stuck to the idea that the biker would lead us to the missing coin. "Jimmy's jeans were tight," she said, "so I don't think the coin could have just slipped out of his pocket. Finding the biker will probably be all the luck we need."

She reached over and took hold of my right arm. She began to rub it and as soon as she did, the muscles in my arm tightened. Surprised by the suddenness of my reaction, she let go of my arm and said, "What's the matter?"

"I get a little nervous when I think I'm going to take my mind off the road," I admitted. "I think it's because of what happened to my father. Anyway, it's not that I don't want you holding my arm."

"I understand," she said seriously. "I think I'd be the same way if something bad happened to anyone in my family in a car accident."

I didn't say anymore. There wasn't anything more to say. My mother had been frightened when I first started driving. She'd tried her best to keep her fear to herself, but sometimes she'd slipped. She wasn't frightened anymore, but through all of that, I'd become very careful at the wheel. The funny thing was that the muscles in my arm had responded automatically.

The same muscles didn't tighten when Sherri took hold of my arm on the way into the Pancake House. My mind turned to what she had said about finding the biker. I hoped she was right. The thought of trying to find the coin at the fair was too much for me, especially on an empty stomach.

A stack of blueberry pancakes took care of my hunger, and Sherri satisfied hers with two eggs and strips of bacon. Over coffee, she provided the directions for our ride to Van Nuys Kawasaki. I didn't bother to tell her that I thought I knew the way. She wanted to be a partner in the whole thing, and I couldn't see any good reason for cooling her interest. She also informed me that she'd talked to Karen and had been annoyed by her friend. "We're doing Karen a favor," she said, "and I had to remind her of that, Terry. She acted as if we were working for her."

"That's the way she is," I suggested. "Hadn't you noticed?"

"I noticed, Terry, but I tried to overlook that thing about her. I like her, even if she does get on my nerves every now and then."

"Well, the coin may be getting on her nerves right now. Her parents don't sound like the nicest people in the world, and even if they were, I don't imagine that they'd be happy to learn they'd lost something worth thousands of dollars. I think she has a lot more to worry about than if she's acting all right."

Sherri reached over and placed her hand in mine. "For a big, tough guy, you're pretty understanding," she said.

"Sure," I said, "so how about paying the check? I understand you want to."

"Right," she said, laughing, "I'm glad you didn't forget."

We rode along the Ventura Freeway west to Van Nuys Boulevard. There we hit the off-ramp. Van Nuys is in the heart of the San Fernando Valley, and the Boulevard is lined with new and used car lots. They are big lots and hidden among them was Van Nuys Kawasaki.

After parking across the street from the showroom, I decided to stay in the car. The cycle people certainly weren't bound to provide any information about their customers, and I figured that the two of us asking questions might provide a big reminder of that fact. Besides, I figured Sherri knew more about bikes and looked better than I did. Both things would help.

I watched as Sherri stepped into the crosswalk and stopped traffic. Two cars driven by young guys screeched to a halt, and I laughed thinking about how they would have raced through the crosswalk if I were standing in it.

I could see a few biker types in the showroom when Sherri entered it. They were wearing leather jackets, even though it was probably 80 degrees in the sunlight. I didn't regard those types as tough, but I was sure they could take the heat better than I could. Maybe, I laughed to myself, the zippers on their jackets were stuck. While they were being helped, Sherri seemed to be browsing around the showroom. The moving traffic obscured my view a little, but I did see her pick up a few pieces of literature which I guessed were for her brother. I wondered if he, too, wore a leather jacket.

A guy who looked young to me was working in the showroom. Several times, I saw his head turn in Sherri's direction, and I guessed he was as anxious to get to her as she was to get some information from him. Finally, he slipped some literature into the hands of the bikers and hustled them out of the showroom. The bikers didn't seem to mind the rush they'd been given. At least, it didn't seem that way from the expression on their faces, but I wasn't sure that their blank looks ever changed.

From the movement of Sherri's hands, I could tell that

she was describing the bike we wanted to know about. I could also see that the Kawasaki guy wasn't paying as much attention to her hands as he should have been, but I couldn't blame him, especially after seeing two of his usual customers.

After a few minutes, the guy led Sherri over to his desk and leafed through some sort of ledger book sitting on top of it. When he found what he was looking for, he handed Sherri his pen and a piece of paper.

I hoped Sherri wasn't getting a bunch of names and addresses, but she finished too quickly for that. The guy followed her to the door, taking in her every step and talking all the time. I halfway wished I could read his lips because I couldn't help wondering if he was coming on to her.

Again, I watched Sherri stop traffic. The smile on her face told me that she'd been successful.

"I got it," she said, sliding back into her seat and closing the car door.

"I thought so," I said, "but here comes your friend."

The Kawasaki guy was dodging cars as he ran across the street toward us. I wished he'd used the crosswalk.

"Hi," he said, trying to catch his breath and thrusting his face into the open window on Sherri's side of the car, "I just thought of something else that you and your brother should know."

Sherri was turning toward the guy and reaching behind her back and touching my arm at the same time. I didn't need the signal. I wasn't about to blurt out that I wasn't her brother. "What is it?" she asked.

"That guy you're looking for rides with a crazy gang," he said. "They get off on playing rotten tricks. He's not too bad when the gang isn't around, so whatever you want to talk to him about, I'd do it when he's alone."

"Hey, thanks a lot," Sherri said. "We won't forget that, will we, Terry?"

I didn't get a chance to answer. "Sherri and Terry," the guy laughed. "That's pretty good for a sister and brother. You don't have another sister named Merry, do you?"

"No," Sherri said, faking a laugh while I started the engine, "but that's a good idea. We're going to have to kid our parents about it. Now you take care and thanks again."

I pulled away. In my rearview mirror, I could see the guy was still grinning about Sherri, Terry, and Merry. "He was real funny," I mumbled.

"Hey," Sherri said, "he was all right. He did give me the biker's name and address."

"He gave us more than that, little sister," I said, half-joking. "He gave us a good reason to separate the biker from his friends."

Looking over at me, Sherri said, "I know."

By the sound of her voice, I knew she was thinking about Jimmy.

6

The address was for a street in North Hollywood. The street crossed Hollywood Way, and I knew the neighborhood. It contained one-family stucco houses.

When we reached the street and parked, I couldn't help thinking that the houses on it resembled houses in certain sections of Glendale, except the North Hollywood houses had more graffiti on them. I never could understand why kids wanted to waste their money on spray paint, but maybe they weren't wasting their money. Maybe they were stealing the paint.

The biker's name was George Tesnick, and it didn't look as if he was home. From what we could see, his bike wasn't. The Tesnick nameplate above the doorbell was old and rusty enough to show that they'd been living there a long time. The lady who answered the bell was old, too. She could have passed for George's grandmother, but she sounded like his mother.

"Why are you looking for my boy George?" she asked

nervously, making me think that only trouble rang for George.

"I've got a bike that he might be interested in," I lied.

"Not George," she said, shaking her head. "He's got a brand new bike. He wouldn't be interested in your bike."

"Well, maybe some of his friends would," I said, trying to sound anxious. "I need to sell it. Do you know where I could find them?"

Some of the suspicion seemed to disappear from the old lady's eyes. "I think George went over to Griffith Park. If he's there, he'll be with his friends. You know him, don't you?"

"Sure I know him," I replied, starting to back away from the door. "I'll go over to Griffith Park now and look for him."

"If you see him, you tell him to be home for dinner," she called after me, "and tell him not to be late."

I nodded and smiled. From what I'd heard about her Georgie boy, I figured she could throw the food into his cage now, but there was no sense in telling her that. She hadn't acted as if Georgie boy made her life very happy.

"You almost made me laugh out loud when you lied like that," Sherri said. "I wished you'd told me what you planned to do."

"I would have if I'd known," I answered. "Anyway, maybe we can find George in the park. At least you know him."

"If the fellow from the Kawasaki shop was right," she said, correcting me, "and if he was, I'm not sure we want to find all of the bikers together."

She was right. Riding over to Griffith Park wasn't the best of ideas. We could have sat around and waited for George to come home for dinner, but there was one big thing wrong with that idea. We didn't know for certain that George was our biker, and Monday morning was getting closer all the time. So we quickly decided to look for George and his friends. With luck, maybe we'd be able to keep out of their way if we found them.

Griffith Park was a short ride from George's home. It's a public park, but to hold down the traffic in it, someone had decided that a parking fee needed to be charged for cars entering the park, even if they weren't parking. It seemed like a stupid idea to me and a lot of other people, but there wasn't much we could do about it except stay out of the park. After I paid the fee, the woman in the toll booth said, "Have a nice day."

"You, too," I said automatically and headed up the road towards the planetarium.

I imagined we'd find bikers somewhere near the planetarium and in a short while, I saw that I was right. "That might be them," I told Sherri, as I guided the car into a parking space.

I wondered if they'd paid the toll or if they'd come in through some wooded area of the park. The question didn't matter. There were other things to think about.

The bikers were off the road—too far off it to get a good look to see if George was one of them. "Let's try to get as close as we can without calling attention to ourselves," I told Sherri, as we climbed out of the car.

The bikers were seated on their bikes, talking to one another. We moved closer, and I hoped Sherri would recognize them.

She didn't have to. Georgie boy had good eyes and a good memory. He spotted Sherri before she said a word about him. "Hey, baby," he called, "can't you live without me?"

Georgie didn't particularly frighten me, but there were eight or nine other Georgies with him. I knew if Georgie had the coin, he wasn't going to turn it over to us in front of his friends. It just didn't seem like the right time or place for a friendly talk with Georgie. "Let's get out of here," I told Sherri.

If she had any other ideas, she kept them to herself. We headed for my car as fast as we could go without running. We probably should have run because the roar of bike engines behind us told me that Georgie and his pals had decided to leave their spot in the woods. And I was sure they weren't trying to get away from us.

We made it to the car with the motorcycles coming up fast behind us. As soon as Sherri was inside, I started my engine and told her to roll up her window. She already started.

By the time I released the emergency brake, the car was surrounded by bikers. "Come out here," George commanded, rolling to a stop by Sherri's window.

"Do you think I should tell him about dinner?" Sherri whispered. I smiled over at her, thinking she had a great sense of humor and a terrible sense of timing. We were in trouble.

"Come out here, baby," George called again.

His voice didn't sound as cheerful as it had the first time. "I guess you'll have to go," I said to Sherri, deciding that two jokers were better than one.

"Are you kidding?" she asked quickly, and just as quickly saw the answer in the smile on my face.

We watched as George rolled his bike off a few feet and set down the kickstand. "Let's turn it over," George told the pack of morons who passed for his friends.

One by one, the other bikers parked and quickly joined him on Sherri's side of the car. In a matter of seconds, the entire gang was busy rocking the car. Sherri rolled toward me and my shoulder slammed against the window on my side. It was easy to see that we weren't going to be in an upright position for long. "Hang on," I told Sherri, slamming my floor shift into reverse gear.

George and his pals didn't notice my move. They were having the time of their simple lives. Through my rearview mirror I could see two bikes parked behind me. I hoped I could knock them out of the way instead of having to roll over them. I popped the clutch, and the car peeled back, burning some good rubber. We hit the bikes hard, and I was pleased to see them slide out of the way before they toppled over. My move surprised George and his boys. They stopped the rocking and turned their attention to the downed bikes.

I quickly shifted into first and headed the car in the direction of couple of the bikers. Sherri let out a scream and covered her eyes. The two bikers jumped aside, and I burned a little more rubber as I raced past them. In a matter of seconds, we were winding down the road away from the planetarium.

I kept my eye on the rearview mirror. "Are they following us?" Sherri finally asked.

"It doesn't look like it," I said. "I guess they're checking the bikes that went down, and I guess they're telling George that he has to pay for the damages."

Sherri breathed a sigh of relief and glanced through the rear window. "I'm glad that's over," she said. "You know, I thought you were going to hit those two guys standing near the front of the car. You really scared me."

"Hitting them never entered my mind," I said. "They don't have a lot in the way of brains, but I was sure they weren't going to try to stop the car with their bodies."

"I guess you're right," Sherri said, "but I don't think there is any sense in trying to get the coin from them."

I laughed. "Don't worry, Sherri, we're not going up against those idiots again. George is the one we want to see and sooner or later, he'll have to go home alone. When that happens, I'll show you how tough he is."

She reached over and touched my arm for a second. "You don't have to show me anything," she said seriously. "I care more about you than I do about that old coin."

"That's good to know," I said cheerfully, "but George isn't going to be any trouble without his clones. If I thought he was I'd stay away from his house, and I'd keep you away from it."

Hearing that, she leaned over and kissed me on the cheek. "I'm sorry," she said after that. "I know you want to keep your mind on the road, but I want you to know I think you're wonderful."

"You're all right yourself," I replied, wondering if my face was red.

I drove over to Glendale and pulled into Ralph's Supermarket parking lot on Brand Avenue. I wanted to see how much damage I'd done to the back of my car. To my surprise, it had held up well. There was a small dent in the trunk, but that was it. The dent wasn't the only one on the car, so I didn't feel too bad about it. If George and his boys had been able to finish what they had started, the car would have looked a whole lot worse. "Karen should pay to have that dent fixed," Sherri suggested.

"I don't think so," I replied, after briefly considering her suggestion. "She didn't force us to go to the park. The best thing to do is forget about it."

It was near noon, so I offered to buy lunch. Sherri wasn't hungry, and I wasn't hungry enough to eat alone, so we decided to skip lunch. "I want to stop at my friend Harry's," I said, as we pulled out of the parking lot. "He's a good guy. I'd like you to meet him."

I was in luck. Harry was heading for his car when I pulled up near the front of his house. He spotted my car and walked toward it. We got out and met him.

"You must be Sherri," he said, extending his hand. "I'm Harry Fong. I am one of Terry's few friends."

"He also likes to make jokes," I told Sherri. "He's actually the *reason* I only have a few friends."

"I don't believe either of you," Sherri replied, "but I think I've seen you around school, Harry."

"Possibly," Harry said, winking at me, "but we all look alike."

"Oh, no," Sherri quickly objected, stopping when Harry and I laughed.

"I told you he likes to make jokes," I explained.

"Not funny," she told Harry smiling at him. "Not funny at all."

"Well," Harry shrugged, "you two didn't come here for jokes anyway. What's happening with your missing coin?"

I quickly told Harry about tracking down George and what had happened near the planetarium. He stepped around to the back of my car and surveyed the damage. "Not bad," he said. "You were lucky, but one thing about what happened bothers me."

"What?" I asked.

"If you had stolen something," Harry said, "wouldn't you be slightly nervous if one of the people who might know about it showed up?"

"Yeah," I said, "I guess I would, but George didn't seem nervous at all."

"No, he didn't," Sherri added.

"Maybe he isn't smart enough to be scared," Harry said. "Or maybe he doesn't have the coin anymore. I was just going to ride over to the mall and hang out for a while. Before that, I'll check a few of the coin shops between here and Van Nuys. If he sold it, I'll let the dealer know that he bought stolen property. What does George look like?"

Sherri volunteered a good description of George, while I thought about what Harry had said. When she was finished, I said, "He really wouldn't be nervous if he never had the coin at all."

Harry grinned. "That's the part I wasn't going to tell you," he said, "but if I find out anything about the coin, I'll catch up with you later. It was nice to meet you, Sherri."

I watched Harry walk off. "The usual place?" I called after him.

"Sure," he said, looking back and smiling at us, "if you don't have anything better to do."

We climbed back into my car. "What was all that usual place stuff about?" Sherri asked.

"On weekend nights, we usually hang around Benjie's after the movies let out."

"Unless you have something better to do?" Sherri said, smiling over at me.

"You got it," I said, smiling back.

"I think you might have something better to do tonight," she announced.

I didn't bother to answer. I was thinking the same thing.

7

It was too early to return to George's neighborhood. From what his mother had told us, he probably wouldn't be home until early evening. So partly to use up some time, we rode up to Karen's house to give her a face-to-face report.

When we pulled into the Greensteads' circular drive, Sherri noticed that Jimmy's car was missing. "It looks as if they went out," she said.

She was wrong. Karen was home. The sound of my tires on the gravel brought her to the front door. She rushed over to my car and before I could open the door, she said, "Did you get it?"

"Not yet," I said, motioning for her to back away so I could get out of the car.

"We'll tell you everything that happened," Sherri said, "and by the way, where's Jimmy?"

Karen looked sad enough to make me believe she was hurting. "He's feeling better," she said. "He called this morning and told me. He said he had some things to do.

He didn't say, but I don't think he's coming up here today."

"Let's go inside," Sherri suggested, taking her friend's arm and leading the way.

Once we were inside, Karen seemed to be glad that we were there with her. She got some Cokes for us and also brought some chips and dip into the den. Then she sat down and smiled sadly at Sherri. "I really don't blame Jimmy," she said. "We weren't getting together again or anything like that. I just wanted him to hang around until this was over. I thought he'd do that, so I just feel a little bad that it turned out this way."

I would have guessed that Sherri was going to make some sympathetic comment, but she fooled me by just nodding her head. I ate some chips. I had other things to worry about.

"Well, that's that," Karen said, showing that she could get by without Jimmy. "Now tell me what's been happening with you two."

Sherri covered most of the ground, and I tossed in a few details. I didn't think that we sounded very hopeful, but Karen needed to be hopeful. "Do you think you'll be able to get the coin from this George?" she asked me.

"If he has it, I'll get it," I said, "but if he doesn't have it, time may be running out for us."

"He'll have it," Karen said, trying hard to convince herself.

Sherri and I didn't object to the idea. Right then, I felt a little sorry for Karen. If she'd made any friends in La Crescenta, they obviously weren't good friends or they would have been there with her. For a brief second, I thought about asking her to come with us when we went back to George's house. It was a bad idea. Riding with us wasn't going to change her life. The best thing I could do for her was find the coin before her parents came home. And from the way things looked, even that would be a miracle.

Sherri turned the conversation to food. Karen hadn't eaten lunch, so she made sandwiches for all three of us and we had some more chips and Coke. By the time we were through, it was three o'clock. George's house was about thirty-five minutes from La Crescenta. In a while, we were going to have to leave.

In a way, I was looking forward to seeing George again. I didn't particularly like bikers, but I never looked for trouble with them. But George had really wanted to wreck my car. Even if he didn't have the coin, I wanted to see him again.

When the time came to leave, Karen followed us to the car. By then, she was almost back to her old self, and I was glad I hadn't asked her to join us. She was busy complaining about Jimmy losing the coin and about her parents going away. I could see that she'd get by. All the things that bothered her would keep her busy.

At the car, Sherri insisted on showing Karen the dent in my car. Karen looked properly sorry and thanked me again for all I'd been doing. I waved to her as we pulled away. She tried to smile, but thoughts of Jimmy and her parents made it difficult.

"Are you mad at me about showing Karen the dent?" Sherri asked.

"I'm mad at George about that," I answered, smiling over at her. "Are you mad at yourself for telling Karen?"

Sherri nodded and smiled back. "I know you said that it

wasn't Karen's fault, but I did think that she might offer to have it fixed. You can at least give me credit for trying."

"Thanks," I replied, though I still didn't care much about the dent.

What I really gave Sherri credit for was doing what she wanted. She'd wanted to make something out of the dent, and she had. As for me, I wanted to make something out of George. He was the one who owed me for the dent in my trunk, and I thought about that as we drove toward North Hollywood.

I parked about six blocks from George's house, even though Sherri protested about having to walk too far. I had some ideas about George. One of them was that he'd run away if he was alone and spotted my car. Most of the so-called bad guys I'd known only liked trouble when they were making it. George didn't strike me as the exception to that rule.

As for Sherri, her complaint about having to walk six blocks stopped as soon as I offered to let her wait for me in the car. She didn't want to miss seeing George again. She didn't like him anymore than I did.

8

On the way to George's house, I decided to call home. We spotted a pay phone by a gas station and I called to announce that I was going to miss another dinner.

Sherri didn't need to call because no one was home at her house. They'd gone off on a camping trip to give her brother a try at riding his new trail bike. Counting the moped, the kid had two bikes already. I couldn't imagine how many he'd have by the time he was old enough for a license, but it sounded as if he got his fair share of attention around Sherri's place.

I was happy for the kid, especially after Sherri informed me that she was taking me to her house for dinner after we were through with Georgie. I didn't argue, but I couldn't help thinking I'd probably never get to see Harry that night.

As soon as I finished my call, Sherri said, "Let's go."

"Not yet," I said, picking up the receiver and hitting the buttons for the information operator. The guy on the other end listened to the name and address I gave him and a second or so later, a recording gave me Georgie's phone number. I wanted to make sure he wasn't home already.

On the second ring, the old lady answered. "May I speak to George Tesnick please," I said, trying to sound like an old man.

"He isn't here right now," the old lady answered, "and who is this?"

"This is the Friends of the Old Bikers' Society," I said, smiling over at Sherri. "We want to thank Mr. Tesnick for his hundred dollar donation. It was very generous of him."

"Are you sure you have the right Tesnick?" the old lady asked, sounding concerned about whether Georgie boy had lost his mind. "I just live here with my son."

"Well, the money came from George Tesnick," I said, and then rattled off the address. "Is he your son?"

"Sounds like it," she said, "and he's going to be sorry when I get my hands on him."

"You be sure to thank him for us," I said, and quickly placed the receiver back on its hook.

Sherri was laughing. "You have some weird sense of humor," she said. "What did George's mother think about that?"

"I'm not sure," I kidded. "She said something about getting her hands on him. So let's go. We don't want her to get to him first."

We continued on, laughing a little. It hadn't been a great joke and in a way, I felt a little bad about fooling the old lady. I didn't feel too bad, though, because I was on my way to a possible fight with her charming son.

When we reached George's street, I spotted a nice safe place for us to keep an eye on things. It was a boarded-up stucco building about three doors from George's house. We settled in next to the porch, hoping that none of the neighbors would call the police to check on us. Being surrounded by a SWAT team wasn't something either of us would have liked, but I didn't figure it was likely. The street didn't have that "Neighborhood Watch" feel to it. Avoiding the police seemed a more likely rule around there and at that moment, I was glad for it.

We waited and jokingly wondered if George had called home and decided to skip dinner. By seven, we were getting restless, but a few minutes later, Georgie boy came roaring down the street. I imagined his dinner must have been awfully cold by then and besides, I planned to get to him before he got to it.

He did what I expected, parking on what was left of the lawn. He liked walking about as much as most of the other people in Southern California. I got a good running jump and hit him just as he was setting his kickstand. He fell to the ground with me on top of him. The bike dropped alongside of us.

"I just want to talk," I whispered, giving him a closeup view of my right fist, "but if you'd rather fight, that's all right with me. We can talk after that."

"Talk," Georgie quickly decided, glancing at his house and showing what might have been concern for his mother, "but not here."

I got up slowly, keeping as close to him as possible. "Don't try running for the house," I warned, guessing what was going on in his small mind. "You'll never make it."

George dusted himself off. Obviously, he couldn't stand the sight of dirt on his leather jacket. "We can talk by the shack," he suggested, motioning to the building we had been waiting next to.

When we reached our talking spot, he didn't seem surprised by Sherri, but unlike that morning, he had nothing cute to say to her. Maybe he'd just lost interest. "Now what's this all about?" he asked, sounding a few notes weaker than tough.

"I think you have a pretty good idea," I said. "So why don't you tell us?"

A puzzled look spread across his face. "There's nothing to tell," he said. "I thought this girl might have come to the park looking for me. I guess I was wrong. That's about it."

"Skip the park," I said, doubling my fist and raising it into George's view. "Tell us about the fair."

"There's not a lot to tell," he answered. "The pink-haired guy at the fair was looking for trouble, so we gave it to him. You ain't his brother, are you?"

"I don't think so," I said, catching Sherri grinning at my response, "but I'm interested. So suppose you go over the details of what you did at the fair and go slow so you don't miss anything."

"Okay," George said, pausing for a moment to think. "The guy said something about the girls not being interested in goons. I think that's what he called us. Anyway, we asked him if he wanted to lose a few teeth. He said that he was willing to fight us over in the stable area. So we walked over to the stable area and all the way there, he was acting like a big man and talking about a fair fight. As soon as we got there, the fight started. After a couple of shots, he was out cold. That's about it."

I didn't bother to say anything about the fair fight part.

I already knew how George and his buddies felt about that sort of thing, but his silence about the missing money and coin puzzled me. He didn't seem as if he was looking to have any information beat out of him. In fact, the look on his face told me that he wanted to get to his cold dinner without any new scratches on his sloppy body. "Where'd you spend the money you took?" I asked.

"What money?" he answered, showing some genuine surprise at my question.

"The money you took from the kid you slobs knocked out," I said.

"I get it now," George said, looking as if he'd come up with the first idea of his life. "You think we took some money from that jerk. Well, you're all wrong about that."

I grabbed George's leather jacket and yanked him close to me. "Don't ever call my friend a jerk!" I screamed into his face. "You and that pack of clowns you hang around with are the jerks. Do you understand that?"

He didn't like what I'd told him, but he nodded anyway. I loosened my grip slightly and he got up the courage to talk. "We don't steal," he said.

"You steal," I said, tightening my grip slightly, "but I'm not here about that. I just want to know what you got at the fair."

"We didn't get a thing," George said, sticking to his earlier claim. "We were afraid that the guy was hurt bad, so we got out of there as quick as we could. You can beat me up if you want, but I can't make up a story about taking something from the guy. I don't even know what was missing."

I released George and watched as he smoothed out his

jacket. He was making sense, and he didn't seem to have the imagination needed to create that sense. I didn't like him one bit, but I believed him.

For a brief moment, I thought about hitting him once for Jimmy and the dent in my trunk. It wasn't a good idea. It wouldn't do a thing for Jimmy or my trunk, and it wouldn't make me bigger. "That's about it," I told George, and a look of gratitude spread across his face. "There's just one other thing. If I were you, I wouldn't tell my buddies about this. You know how they are. They'll want to come after me. You know, gang up on me. If that happens, I'll come after you. First I'll get hurt, and then you'll get hurt."

I couldn't read George's blank stare, but he must have been considering what I'd said because he soon smiled and nodded. "You don't say anything," he said, making sure that Sherri understood that she was being included in the arrangement, "and I won't say anything. We just talked, and that's no reason to rumble."

"It's a deal," I said, not bothering to shake George's hand.

George guessed that he was free to go and lost no time in taking advantage of that fact.

I watched him race for his front door. His mother must have spotted his bike on the lawn because she was waiting at the door for him. He was through with us, but he had some explaining to do about his big donation. My guess was that he wasn't getting any dinner.

"Let's get out of here," I said to Sherri.

We started the long walk to my car. We'd spent most of the day on George, and we didn't seem to be any closer to finding the coin. I was beginning to think that we didn't have enough time.

9

"I thought he was telling the truth," I said, as we continued our walk through the streets of North Hollywood.

"I didn't want to," Sherri said, "but I think he was. You really scared him. When you screamed at him, you scared me."

I laughed. "I didn't mean to scare you," I said, "but I knew that screaming would scare him. You have to act a little crazy around guys like George. It gets their attention."

Sherri laughed. "It sure does, and I'm glad you were acting. Now what are we going to do, Terry?"

"Are you kidding?" I said. "We are going to eat, aren't we?"

"Sure," she said, "I just meant what are we going to do about finding the coin?"

"I don't know," I admitted, "but once we fuel up, I'll think of something."

I was glad to see the car. We headed for Glendale and instead of taking the freeway, I stuck to side streets. We weren't far from her house and on Saturday nights, there were more drunks than usual on the freeways. My mother's stories about my father's death had made me cautious about driving.

As we rode, I tried to explain to Sherri why I hadn't taken the freeway. "I'm surprised you drive at all," she said sincerely. "I don't know if I'd be able to."

"I guess you would," I answered. "From what I've been able to learn about my father, I think he would have wanted me to drive. What happened to him was a rotten thing, but it happens to a lot of people. My mom worries a little about my driving, but she never once discouraged me. In fact, I don't think she worries much more than any other mother. She's okay."

Our conversation turned to Sherri's family. Her father was an accountant, and her mother had been a teacher. Now that Sherri and her brother were able to get along by themselves, her mother was thinking about going back to teaching, but she was a little hesitant. She'd read too many news stories about teachers being attacked in schools. Sherri and I grinned a little about that. No teachers had ever been attacked in our classes, though we both agreed that some of them needed to be tried for attempting to murder students by boring them to death.

By the time we reached Sherri's house, my mind had flipped back to the coin. The fair seemed our next likely place to look, but it would be a miracle if we just happened upon the person who found the coin. I climbed out of the car, hoping that Sherri had planned on something better than a TV snack for dinner.

She had. The dinner turned out great, though Sherri

credited most of it to her mother's microwave oven. We had roast beef, corn, and mashed potatoes. After that, we had some ice cream from Baskin-Robbins and coffee. I was full and tired, but I helped with the dishes. I put them into the dishwasher.

While doing that, I thought of some other little point about the missing coin and sprung the idea on Sherri. "What about the stable girls?" I said. "You know, the ones who found Jimmy. Didn't they have the time to take the money and the coin?"

"Oh, I guess they had the time," Sherri answered, "but they didn't seem the type. I mean, why would they steal from him and help him at the same time?"

"I know," I said, "but things like that happen sometimes. Maybe they took the money and the coin and then got frightened. Or maybe they just wanted to make sure he was all right. I think something like that could have happened, especially if it was the first time they ever stole anything."

"Well, I don't think that happened, but I'd know them by sight if we could find them. Would you mind if I put on some warmer clothes before we go?"

I couldn't believe my ears. "Wait a minute," I said, grinning at her. "We're not going out to Pomona at this time of night. The stable girls probably went home long ago. They're around during the day when the races are being run. Then they'll either be at the stables or at the track watching the races. I'm sure they don't hang around the horses day and night."

Sherri was convinced. She called Karen and shared latest developments with her. Karen, according to Sherri, wasn't upset about the bad news concerning George. It sounded as if Karen was getting ready to face her father, but I didn't mention that to Sherri. We still had a little time and some new suspects.

We settled on the couch and watched some television. After a while, we forgot about the television and settled on getting to know each other better. It was late when I departed—too late to look for Harry.

During the drive home, I tried to get my mind on the missing coin, but I wasn't interested in coins at the moment. Sherri was on all the channels, so I just decided to go with the program for a while.

By the time I reached my house, I'd gone over the idea that it had been a good thing for me that the coin had been lost. The bad part of that idea was it brought on memories of Jimmy's eye. Sure Sherri was nice, but finding the coin was the important thing.

My mom had gone to bed, but she'd left a note on the kitchen table for me. It read: "Harry called and told me to give you this message—'No Luck.' He said you'd know what he meant. I hope you do, and I hope I see you in the morning. Love, Mom."

In a way, I was glad Harry hadn't had any luck. Maybe we'd find the coin after all. Then I read the note again and laughed. Maybe Benjie's had run out of rice pudding. It wasn't a bad joke, but it was too late to call Harry and tell it to him. Besides, he wouldn't have laughed.

10

The next morning, I ate breakfast at home with my mother. She was curious to know what was keeping me away from my workouts. I told her most of what had happened, but I avoided telling her about our little run-in by the planetarium and the dent in my trunk. Car things worry her.

After that, she gave me my weekly payment for taking care of the lawn, bushes, garbage, and a few other things around the house. It wasn't much of a job and the pay wasn't too hot, but I could do most of the work when I wanted to do it. In fact, I was behind on most of it. "I'll hit the lawn Monday or Tuesday," I said.

"You do it when you can," my mother said cheerfully, "as long as it's before Wednesday."

I laughed and headed for the phone. I wanted to catch Harry before he went out. He seemed glad to hear from me, though he was sorry he hadn't had any luck with the coin dealers. I told him what had happened with George.

"It'll take a miracle to find the coin between now and your deadline," Harry concluded.

"Thanks for the words of inspiration," I said sarcastically. "I knew I could count on you for them, but let me tell you my idea about the stable girls."

When I finished telling Harry my plan to go to the fair, Harry surprised me. "Three of us can do better than two," he said.

"That's a great idea," I said. "I was thinking about asking you, but I figured you wouldn't go."

"I don't have anything better to do," Harry said, "and besides, I have a way with stable girls."

"Sure," I said laughing, "I'll pick you up in a couple of minutes, and then we'll get Sherri."

I was glad Harry wanted to ride out to the fair. I really wanted to find the coin, but it wasn't going to be as easy as I'd thought the day before. With Harry along, my chances improved.

Sherri was waiting outside when I pulled up with Harry. She was wearing jeans and she'd taken her hair out of the pony tail. It fell over her T-shirt which was light and had no lettering. She was wearing a big smile as she headed for my car, but it faded slightly when she spotted Harry. "I think she wanted to be alone with you," Harry whispered. "She loves your muscles."

"This is almost like alone," I joked back.

"Hi," Harry said to her, getting out of the car, "Terry needed some expert help, so I volunteered to come along. I'll sit in the back."

Sherri smiled at him. "We can use help," she said, "but let me sit in the back. There's not much room back there."

"Okay," Harry said, pushing the passenger seat forward, "but it doesn't make any difference to me."

After Sherri climbed into the back seat, Harry hopped back in and I headed for the eastbound entrance to the freeway. "Do you know your way around the stables?" Sherri asked.

"Did you tell her that?" Harry jokingly asked me.

"I didn't mean anything wrong by that," Sherri quickly said. "I was just wondering about the expert help."

"Oh," Harry said, turning and smiling at her, "I was just kidding about that. I might be able to help, but I'm no expert about anything, especially stables."

"He's an expert at chess," I said.

"Are you?" Sherri asked, showing a sign of real interest. "I love that game."

"Well, I'm pretty good at it," Harry replied, making me smile at his false modesty.

Sherri seemed to know a little about the game, and they talked on as I slid into an eastbound lane and pushed down on the gas pedal. In light traffic, the ride to Pomona was about forty minutes, but the Sunday morning traffic was heavy. I hoped it would ease once we got through Pasadena. I was anxious to get to the fair.

By the time we reached Arcadia, the traffic had eased slightly and it looked as if we'd reach the fair in almost forty minutes. "We're getting closer," Harry remarked, "so let's think about the stable girls. Do you remember what they looked like, Sherri?"

She didn't remember too well, but she described them as best she could. "That's all I remember," she finally said, "but I'll be able to point them out to you."

"That's true," Harry said, but from his response I gathered that he'd been thinking about the three of us splitting up and saving time in the search for the girls.

"There are only two places they might be," I told him.

"There are only two places you thought of," he corrected me. "There are a thousand places to be at the fair."

I didn't bother to answer, but he was right. I wished Sherri remembered the stable girls as well as she remembered George and his bike. Still it didn't make a big difference because if the stable girls had the coin, it might be better if three of us confronted them.

When we reached the fairgrounds exit, I could tell by the traffic that the fair was going to be crowded. The traffic slowed to a crawl and we inched our way toward the parking lot.

About ten minutes later, I parked and we started the long walk to the admission booth. There I offered to pay for all of us, but Harry and Sherri insisted on paying for themselves. I was glad for that, though the idea of billing Karen had passed through my mind when I made the offer. The trouble was I didn't think she'd pay.

Harry checked with one of the ticket takers and learned that the horse races didn't start until 12:30. "So we go to the stables," he said.

Sherri led the way. She showed us where she and Karen had come upon Jimmy and the stable girls. From that starting point, we moved from stable to stable and through all the nearby walking areas.

The whole stable area was busy, and many girls were working with horses. Unfortunately, Sherri didn't recognize one of them, though by then she was certain she would recognize the girls if we came upon them. Finally, Sherri said, "Let's ask somebody about them. Maybe my descriptions aren't as bad as I thought. It's worth a try."

"I don't think so," I said, looking over at Harry. "If the girls took the coin and they find out that somebody is looking for them, they're not going to stick around to find out who it is. I think we should look for them over at the racetrack. The races will be starting soon."

"I'm not sure they'd run away," Harry said. "After all, they're working here. People must be looking for them every day."

"That's right," Sherri said, almost gloating over the fact that Harry seemed to be taking her side.

"But still we should look for them over at the racetrack," Harry told her, "because your descriptions are as bad as you thought."

"That's right," Sherri said again, but this time she didn't turn my way. "Let's go."

When we reached the racetrack, I couldn't believe my eyes. People were packed into it like there was going to be a rock concert. "I didn't think so many people went to the races," I said to Harry.

"It's always crowded," Harry said. "I think my Uncle Tom is here. If you spot him, tell me."

I knew Harry's uncle. He had a dry cleaning store in Glendale. "Who's at the store?" I asked.

Harry laughed. "My aunt. She's there every Sunday. She hates the races."

From what I could see, there were about 20,000 people at the track, and the grandstand seemed to have seating for about 10,000 of them. According to Harry, the races lasted through most of the remaining daylight hours, so it looked as if many of the people were getting ready for a long stand.

We stood and watched, while Harry tried to explain the big computerized betting board to me. I didn't know much about betting on horses, but if most of the people were getting rich by doing it, they were dressing to keep that fact a secret. They didn't even look happy, and the races hadn't even started yet.

"The race track is like life," Harry remarked. "Not many poor people get rich here, and not many rich people get poor."

"Where does that leave your uncle?" I asked.

"Cleaning clothes five days a week," Harry laughed.

"Are we just going to stand here and stare at the people?" Sherri asked.

"No," Harry answered quickly, "what we need to do is work our way through the crowd here and in the infield. After that, we can work our way through the grandstand. That isn't totally systematic, but it seems to be the best we can do."

It took us almost an hour to push our way through half of the crowd in front and off to the side of the grandstand. It was boring work and it was hot. "How about stopping for something to eat?" I asked, as the horses paraded past for the start of the third race.

"I'm just thirsty," Sherri said. "How about you, Harry?"

He was hungry, so the three of us went to a refreshment stand underneath the grandstand. It was as crowded in there as it was outside. Some people were making bets, while others were getting ready to watch the race on TV monitors. Sherri had a lemonade, and I had one, too, along with a plate of chips covered with melted cheese. Harry had a hot dog and a Coke.

While we were eating, the third race was run. A horse named My Little Dolly got out in front and from what the people watching the monitors were saying, they wanted another horse to win. The race ended in a little over a minute, and My Little Dolly stayed in front all the way. The people groaned. "Didn't anyone bet on that horse?" I asked Harry.

"Look up there," Harry said, pointing at another computerized betting board. "My Little Dolly was number 5. The '40' next to the number 5 up there means she's going to pay over $80 for a $2 bet to win. She was a longshot. That means that not many people bet on her."

"We're longshots, too," Sherri said. "Not many people would bet we're going to find those stable girls."

"Not standing here," I said, thinking a little about trying to make a bet on the next race. "Let's get going."

As we were walking through the tunnel that led to the area in front of the grandstand, I spotted a man who looked familiar. "Hey, Harry," I said, pointing, "I think that's your Uncle Tom."

"I think you're right," Harry said. "Wait here. I'll be right back."

I pulled Sherri over to the wall, out of the way of the crowd moving back and forth through the tunnel. "That was lucky, wasn't it?" I said to her.

"Yes, it was," she said sadly.

I could see that she was tired and losing faith in our ability to find the stable girls. I tried to think of something to say to cheer her a little, but I was getting tired, too. The man making the announcements over the public address system came on and said that My Little Dolly had paid $83.60 to win. He went on to say some more numbers and something else about the second and third horses, but the crowd was roaring over the winning price. "Did you see that pig win?" a man standing nearby said to another man.

I laughed. "Now that wasn't a nice thing to say about My Little Dolly," I whispered to Sherri.

Smiling back at me, she said, "I don't think he bet on her."

Several more minutes passed, and I found myself wishing that Harry would hurry. It was cool in the tunnel, but I was anxious to get on with our search. Sherri must have been reading my mind. "I hope he comes back soon," she said, leaning against me.

I was about to answer when I spotted Harry pushing his way through the crowd. "Here he comes," I told Sherri, taking her hand and moving toward Harry.

"I was telling my uncle what we were doing here," Harry said as soon as he reached us.

"What'd he say?" I asked.

Harry frowned. "He said that we're wasting our time."

"That's great," Sherri said.

"Yes and no," Harry said. "He reminded me that the crowd keeps shifting. Some people leave. Other people take their seats. Other people who have been sitting decide to stand. So, like he said, it's really impossible to come close to checking the crowd. He said that we'd have a better chance in the stable area. I think he's right."

"What do you think?" Sherri asked me.

I looked at Harry. "Is your uncle winning?"

"He sure is," Harry said. "He had a $10 bet on My Little Dolly."

"I think we should go to the stable area," I told Sherri.

She glanced at Harry and saw the big smile on his face. "You guys are crazy," she said, and a big smile spread across her face, "but let's go."

11

The stable area wasn't as busy as it had been before the start of the races, but still there was a lot of activity. Again, we started to move from stable to stable, but this time we were stopped by a security guard. "What are you doing?" he asked.

"We're looking for a couple of stable girls we know," I said.

"You can check for them at the stable offices," he said, "but you have to stay outside that fence over there. Only stable people are allowed in this area."

"We were here before the races," Sherri said.

The guard shrugged. "You weren't supposed to be," he said. "I'm sorry, but that's the way it is."

While the guard watched, we moved to the outside of the metal link fence. "What a pain," Sherrri remarked.

"It's no big thing," Harry said. "We can still see all the stables and the walking areas. If the girls are here, we'll see them."

Harry was right, but we didn't see them and by the time we reached the last row of stables, I was thinking about calling the search off. An old man who was rubbing down a hot horse caught my eye. He looked old enough to know everybody who worked in the stable area. "Hey, mister," I called to him through the fence, "could you help us?"

He dropped his sponge into the pail of water and tied the horse to a walker. Then he approached the fence. "How can I help you?" he asked.

"We're looking for some stable girls," I answered. "She can describe them."

"No sense in doing that," the old man said. "I don't pay that much attention to stable girls. They come and they go. A lot of them are lazy, no lazier than the boys, but lazy. Stable work is hard work. It's not for lazy people."

"He's not lazy," Harry remarked, pointing at me.

"No, he doesn't look it," the old man said, and then turned his attention back to me. "You look strong, boy, but your muscles are getting too tight from weightlifting. Surprised you, didn't I? You probably didn't think an old man like me could see that you lifted weights. Well, I might smell a little like a horse, but I'm a little smarter than I smell. Why are you looking for the girls?"

"They helped a friend of ours a few days ago," I said. "We wanted to ask them about what happened."

"Well, I hope you find them," the old man said and started to turn away. "I have to get back to work."

"Pink hair," Harry blurted out.

The old man turned, and we saw a big smile on his face. "Why didn't you say that in the first place?" he asked. "Those girls who helped the pink-haired fellow are over at Santa Anita. Racing starts over there in a few days. The girls took a lot of kidding about helping that fellow. Stable people don't go for pink hair. I'm surprised that fellow is a friend of yours. Is he crazy?"

"A little bit," I answered, "but are the girls working now?"

The old man pulled a gold pocket watch from inside his shirt and looked at it. "If you hurry, they might still be there," he said, "but mornings are better. Go tomorrow after sunup."

"That'll be too late," I said. "We'll go now. Thanks for your help, Mr. . . . ?"

"Just make it boy," he said, winking at us. "The oldest stable boy in California and you met him right here at the fairgrounds."

"Well, thanks again," Harry said, and the three of us headed for my car.

"It was a good thing you thought of pink hair," Sherri told Harry.

"I know," he replied, smiling over at me. "It was one of those expert things I came along for."

"So was searching the crowd," I joked back.

By my guess, Santa Anita Racetrack was about twenty miles from the fairgrounds. We'd passed the exits for Santa Anita on the way to the fair. The track was in Arcadia. It was a big racetrack, and I wasn't even sure where the stables were situated, but that was the least of our worries. First, we had to get there on time. Then we had to find the stables.

Once we were back on the freeway, I pushed down on the gas pedal until the needle said that we were going sixty-five. Plenty of cars were breezing by us, so I figured we were safe from being stopped by the Highway Patrol. I wasn't certain, though, because the Highway Patrol seems to have a special interest in young drivers in sporty cars. My Capri, dents and all, was sporty enough for the Highway Patrol, but with time going against us, I had to risk a ticket.

We reached Arcadia in about fifteen minutes and exited onto Baldwin Avenue. Sherri said that she thought the stable area was just north of the Santa Anita Mall on Baldwin. Harry and I had no idea, so we followed Sherri's lead.

Cruising down Baldwin, I spotted a track entrance sign with "stable area" printed below it. To the west of us, the sun looked like it was getting ready to drop into the ocean. It was late. I parked in the lot next to the stable area, hoping it wasn't too late.

There were about two dozen cars parked in the lot, and it looked as if some people were starting to leave for home. The three of us hopped out of the car and looked toward the stable area. Two uniformed security guards were leaning against what seemed to be a guard shack. "Might as well wait here," I said. "If the girls are in there, they'll be coming out this way. If they aren't in there, we'll know as soon as all the cars are gone."

"Not if some people sleep in the stables," Harry remarked.

He was right, but I didn't bother to acknowlege the fact. I could tell by the worried look on Sherri's face that she agreed with him.

About ten minutes later, Sherri pointed at two girls walking by the security guards. "There they are," she said excitedly.

The girls were headed for a Datsun pickup parked about

a hundred feet from us. One of the girls had long black hair, and the other had stringy blonde hair. They were both about the same size. The three of us headed for them.

The black-haired girl recognized Sherri right away. "Hey, how are you?" she said, smiling. "Is that punker fellow all right?"

"He's fine," Sherri replied. "His eye seemed bad for a while, but he's doing all right now."

"Were you looking for us?" the stringy blonde asked, directing the question at me.

"Sort of," I said, trying to think of a polite way to ask the rotten question I had to ask and deciding there was no nice way. "The fellow who got hurt lost some money that day, and I was wondering if you saw anything of it?"

The blonde didn't try to hide her disgust. "Now what kind of question is that?" she asked, without waiting for an answer. "Why would we see money on the ground and leave it there? If you're trying to say that we took some money from that guy, say it."

"Listen," I said, "we're not interested in the money. The guy lost something else. That's what we're interested in."

Before the blonde could reply, the dark-haired girl turned to Harry and said, "Your friend with the muscles sure has a nice way of putting things. We can keep the money if we tell you about the other thing, whatever it is. Do you know what we did? We helped the poor slob. We didn't take his money. We didn't take the other thing. We just did what we shouldn't have done. We forgot to mind our own business."

"No," Harry told her, "you did right, and you have to understand that we're doing the same thing. The punker lost a valuable coin, and we're just trying to help him find it. We're not trying to say that either of you did anything."

Both girls stared hard at Harry. I couldn't blame them for being angry. I couldn't be sure, but I would have bet that they had nothing to do with the missing coin. "I didn't mean to come on to you like that," I said. "I'm sorry."

"Okay," the blonde said, "just forget about it. We didn't see any coin or any money."

We watched as the stable girls climbed into their truck. A few seconds later, the engine roared and they drove off, spraying some gravel on the three of us. I turned to Sherri, and I could see that she was close to crying. "I didn't handle that very well," I said, trying to apologize.

"It's not you," she said, and walked off.

I looked at Harry. "Go ahead and talk to her," he said. "I'll be waiting in the car."

When I caught up with Sherri, she moved close to me and said, "Just hold me for a minute, will you?"

I held her tight and she cried hard. After a while, she stepped back and brushed her eyes. They were streaked with red lines. "I was just feeling bad for you," she said. "You've been trying so hard and that seemed like such a lousy ending. I wanted to hit that girl when she talked to you like that, but I could see that it wasn't her fault. The whole thing's just a mess and I probably should have kept you out of it, so I'm sorry."

I hugged her again and she shed a few more tears. "Come on," I finally said, taking her hand. "Harry must be starving to death. A little food will be good for all of us. It's been a bad day."

When we reached the car, we saw that Harry was sitting

in the back seat. "I'm sorry to keep you waiting," Sherri said to him. "I just got upset."

"If the girls did not come, we'd still be waiting," Harry said. "Then I'd be upset. It happens to all of us."

To my surprise, Sherri smiled slightly. I didn't know why, but I was glad to see it. "Where are we going to eat?" I said, and started the engine.

"I'm going to Karen's," Sherri said. "Will you take me there?"

"Okay," I said, halfway wondering if she was angry with me.

We rode a few blocks in silence until Harry said, "Has he been telling you that all I eat is rice pudding?"

Sherri and I laughed. Then she said, "I'd really rather go and eat with you two, but we can do that some other time. Karen needs me now. Once she finds out that we couldn't find the coin, she's not going to be as cool as she tries to act. It'll all sink in. Her father's not the nicest guy in the world. He won't be happy telling her only one time that she was foolish about the coin. No, he's going to hound her the same way he used to hound her about Jimmy. I think I should eat with her and stay with her as long as I can tonight. Does that make sense to you?"

"Yes," I said, wishing that I'd been able to find that damn coin, "it makes a lot of sense. Harry and I can come back and pick you up later on if you want us to?"

"No, I'll get a ride from my father," she said, and turned to Harry. "You understand, don't you?"

"Sure," he replied.

By the time I pulled into the Greensteads' drive, the three of us were talking about school the next day. It wasn't the most interesting thing to talk about, but it had lightened the air. "Want to meet Karen?" Sherri asked Harry.

"Some other time," he said. "I'll look for you in school tomorrow."

I got out of the car and walked with Sherri toward Karen's front door. "If your father can't come for you," I said, "call me at home. I'll probably be in early."

"I will," Sherri said, "and thanks."

Before I could say another word, she leaned over and kissed my cheek. Then she turned to go. "I'll see you," I said.

Harry had climbed into the front seat. I got in behind the wheel and saw Sherri step inside Karen's house. "I wish we'd found that coin," I said to Harry.

"Are you giving up?" he asked.

"Why?" I said. "Did you think of something?"

"I can't think on an empty stomach," he replied.

I pushed in the clutch and cranked the engine. It was nice to have a good friend like Harry. I didn't think we had a chance in the world of finding the coin, but Harry knew me. I didn't want to give up.

12

For no particular reason, we decided to eat at an Italian restaurant on Verdugo Road in Montrose. It was the first time either of us had eaten in the place and by the time we finished our salads, we knew we'd never eat there again.

As we picked at the lasagna we'd ordered, Harry said, "How'd you happen to pick this place?"

"A friend of mine liked the looks of it," I answered jokingly and gestured toward his plate. "I thought you were hungry."

Harry grinned at me. "About as hungry as you are," he said.

Five minutes later, we dropped more than enough money on the table and took off. We didn't want to wait and run the risk of having our waitress offer to put the leftovers into doggie bags.

"I think I'm going home," Harry announced as soon as we climbed back into the car.

"How come?" I asked, wondering what was bothering him.

"I'm supposed to call some girl tonight," he explained. "Anyhow, I want some quiet time to think about the missing coin. Can you stop by later?"

"Sure," I said. "I'll drop you off and drive around for a while."

We rode south on Verdugo Road and in a few minutes, we were in Glendale. "Hey," Harry said, "why didn't you introduce me to Karen? Doesn't she like Asians?"

I knew he was kidding, so I said, "She only likes Japanese guys. You'd never be able to pass. Japanese guys hate rice pudding."

Harry laughed. "Wrong," he said, "they like raw rice pudding. They have pudding bars in Japan. They'll have them in LA soon."

"Yeah," I laughed, "but you'll still be going to Benjie's."

"And you'll still be following me there," he joked back.

I turned onto Harry's street and pulled up in front of his house. "I'm just going to ride around for a while," I said.

"I knew you would," he said. "Don't forget to come by later."

When Harry reached his front door, he turned and waved. I waved back and shifted into first. I let up on the clutch and headed for Los Feliz Boulevard. I, too, needed some time to think.

I drove south and thought about all the things that had happened since Friday afternoon. I couldn't think of anything I'd done wrong, except for the way I'd talked to the stable girls. Perhaps they'd fooled me, but if they had, they didn't belong at Santa Anita. They belonged at MGM or one of the other movie studios. The damn coin was probably covered by dirt under some ride at the fairgrounds.

After Los Feliz twisted into Western Avenue, I continued south until I reached Hollywood Boulevard and turned right onto it. The bright lights up ahead of me signaled what some people called "The Heart of Hollywood." Other people used other body parts to describe the area.

About fifteen minutes later, I found a parking space. Even though it was a Sunday night, the Boulevard was crowded with tourists, locals, and what the people of Glendale called "freaks." The so-called freaks were any people who looked or dressed a little different from the average fifty-year-old in Glendale.

The sidewalk on the Boulevard is lined with stars, and each star bears the name of a big shot in the entertainment field. Most of the people named on the stars are dead, but each year new stars are added. The stars draw the tourists who read the names as they walk and probably memorize them for their trivia quizzes.

I stopped by a star in front of an orange drink stand. The name on it was Al Jolson. He'd starred in the first talking movie. In a way, he'd started the whole thing. Some black gum spots covered part of his star. I wondered how he'd feel about that if he could see it, and I decided he'd probably laugh. Hollywood was meant for laughs.

The orange drink stand had only one customer, but the guy who waited on me acted as if it was crowded. He sounded like a New Yorker, but I didn't bother to ask him. I wasn't really interested and besides, his orange juice was lousy.

When I stepped out onto the street again, one tourist was telling another some kind of story about Al Jolson. So much for worrying about black gum spots.

The crowds on the Boulevard had thinned a little, but the area still looked like Dodger Stadium compared to what I would find on Brand Boulevard in Glendale at that time of night. Except for the movie theaters, Glendale closed at about six on the days that it was open. Five minutes later, I was sick of the crowds and heading for my car. Some of Glendale had rubbed off on me, but not all of it.

Fifteen minutes later, I was cruising up Brand Boulevard in Glendale. It was as dead as it was supposed to be. The Crown Bookstore had two people in it. They worked there. I passed a magic store, and a little blinking sign in its window read "Trick Coins." I couldn't help laughing at that sign, wishing that one of them could turn into the one I wanted.

Finally, I twisted my radio dial to a better brand of rock and turned my car in the direction of Harry Fong's house. I hoped he hadn't changed his mind and gone out. When I reached his street, I felt lucky for the first time that day. He was home.

"I'm glad you came back," Harry said, leading me into his room.

I sat down on his bed, propping my head and back against the headboard. "You don't mind if I make myself at home, do you?" I joked.

Harry sat at his desk and twisted in the chair to face me. "Where'd you go?" he asked.

I told him and as soon as I reached the point about driving to his house, he said, "How about a cold drink?"

"I could use one," I replied, reminding myself about the orange juice.

He was back in a minute with two cans of Coke. "Thanks," I said, flipping open the lid on my can and gulping down a few ounces. "That tasted good."

Harry sipped on his soda. He seemed to be studying me. "All right," I finally said, "tell me what you think I did wrong."

"Not much," he said, "but next time you're working out on a Friday don't stop to answer the door."

I laughed and Harry laughed, too. Right then, I thought that he would have made a great brother. "You're all right," I told him. "You're a little too smart, but you're all right."

"You're getting better yourself," he said. "I think Sherri is about the best person to lead you into trouble in a long time."

I laughed again and drank the rest of my Coke. "What were you thinking about before I got here?" I asked.

"I was wondering how many years it would take to burn all of the world's coal reserves." Harry replied in all seriousness.

"How many?"

"I can't get it," Harry said cheerfully. "It's something like the search for the coin. Some of the facts are missing."

I grinned because I'd expected Harry to be thinking about something as crazy as the thing he was thinking about. "Did you get any facts from the girl you called?" I said jokingly.

Harry laughed out loud. "Sure," he said. "Among other

unimportant things, she told me that she wears a bracelet with a name and address on it. And she told me that it was the neatest thing she owned."

"Is there something wrong with her health?" I asked.

"She doesn't think so," Harry said, grinning. "I asked her a couple of times, but she doesn't think so."

"You certainly manage to find bright girls," I said.

We laughed and talked for a while longer. Finally, it was time to go home, but I couldn't help thinking that Harry was holding back on something—something that might help me find the coin.

He walked me to the front door and as we passed the living room, I waved to his mother and father. They were watching television. "They won't wave back," Harry whispered. "They're hooked on the tube. They only bother me when there's a power blackout."

"That's not nice," I whispered back.

"I know," he agreed, as we stepped outside. "I think the girl I called makes me like that. Her bracelet is destroying my mind."

"Did you give up on chess?" I asked, thinking of Harry's mind.

"Of course not," Harry answered, "but my electronic partner failed me, and I had to send it out to be fixed. It was making moves before the game started. That wasn't very sportsmanlike for a machine. Now how do you like that? Making moves before the game started. You think about that."

"Sure," I said, "I'll stay up all night thinking about that."

"Just some of the night," Harry called after me.

I was home five minutes later, but Harry's cryptic goodbye was stuck in my head. My mother had left a note, telling me she was out and might be home late. I tried to remember if I had any homework due on Monday. I couldn't think of any.

It was a long time before I settled into bed and closed my eyes. I spent the time wishing I had found the coin. I was also wishing Harry hadn't filled my head with mysterious talk. I needed some sleep.

13

I may have needed sleep, but I didn't get much that night. Every little dream seemed to be a nightmare about that rotten coin. I'd awaken and try to turn my mind to something else, but then Harry's little message kept popping up. Suddenly, the answer to the puzzle hit me. I rolled over and looked at my alarm clock. It was almost 3:30 in the morning. Answer or not, it was a terrible time to be getting up.

I moved through the house as quietly as I could. I couldn't find the phone book and I finally gave up my search for it. Calling information was the next best thing to having a phone book.

The information operator gave me the bad news I sort of expected. He said that the Greensteads' phone was unlisted and from the sound of his voice, I decided that it wasn't any sense to tell him it was an emergency.

I showered and dressed as fast as I could. Then I scratched out a short note for my mother and dropped it on the kitchen table. It said that I'd left early. I knew she'd be able to guess that anyway, but I didn't want her to think I was losing my mind.

There wasn't a soul on the northbound Glendale Freeway, not even a California Highway Patrol Car. Still I kept my speed below the legal limit. The Highway Patrol has a way of appearing from nowhere, and I didn't need any speeding tickets to go along with my dented trunk.

When I pulled into the drive, I could see a few lights on in Karen's house, but I didn't think she was up yet. I figured that she was like a lot of other people. She'd left the lights on for protection. There was no sense in making the burglars trip over everything. They might get angry.

I played a number on the doorbell, and the chimes inside played one back. Finally, I heard some movement inside the house. I stood in front of the viewer set in the door and waited, guessing that Karen was on the other side checking me out. Then the door opened slightly and she said, "Terry, what are you doing here? Did something happen to Sherri?"

"No," I said, pushing my way into the house, "but I need your help."

She was wearing a short nightgown—not the sort of thing for answering the door. "I need to get my bathrobe," she said quickly.

"Forget it," I told her. "Nothing shows, and I promise not to describe your nightgown to a soul."

After looking down and checking the gown, she smiled. "Okay," she said, "but what kind of help can I give you?"

"You can try hard to remember where Jimmy lived in Ohio," I answered.

She didn't have to think hard. "That's easy," she said. "He lived in Brooklyn. The Dodgers came from there."

Where she picked up that last little bit of information would have been interesting to know, but I didn't bother to ask her about it. I just hoped she was right about Brooklyn, and I just hoped there was one in Ohio. "Where's the nearest phone?" I said, peering into the living room. She led me to the den and searched around for a paper and pencil. While she was doing that, I said, "Did Jimmy ever mention his father's first name?"

Karen laughed. "He sure did," she said. "It's Nat. Jimmy used to call him 'The Fly.' You know, like a gnat."

I tried to smile. In addition to having a great hairstyle, Jimmy was funny. Once she gave me the paper and pencil, I tried to get through to Ohio for information, hoping that Brooklyn wasn't another one of Jimmy's jokes. It wasn't. There was a Brooklyn, and there was a Nathaniel Thompson living in it. There wasn't a single Nat and though Karen might have laughed, I didn't bother to ask about flies. I wrote down Nathaniel Thompson's phone number. Maybe, just maybe, it was the number I wanted.

"This call's on your old man," I told Karen as I dialed the number. "Tell him you don't know anything about it and let him fight it out with the phone company."

Karen half-smiled. She was puzzled and I couldn't blame her, but there was no time for explanations. It was close to five and if I had the right number, I needed to catch Jimmy's father before he left for work. I knew it was later in Ohio, but I didn't know if it was two or three hours later.

On the third ring, a man answered. He sounded groggy. "Mr. Thompson," I said, "this is William Berger. Would you tell Jimmy that I've located the coins he wanted."

There was a long pause on the other end and Karen

gasped at my end. From the silence, I figured that I'd just wasted a phone call, but Nat Thompson finally came through. "Jimmy's not living here anymore," he said. "He's in Glendale, California, at his grandmother's place. I can give you the number, but I think you'd be wasting your time and money. The kid sold all those coins of his before he left here. He's got pink hair now, so do you want the number?"

"Pink hair," I repeated, trying not to laugh. "No, no, I don't think I'll take the number, Mr. Thompson. Thanks anyway, and I'm sorry to hear that your boy left."

Nat Thompson must have hated pink hair. "I'm not," he answered.

I put down the receiver and smiled at Karen. "I think I'm going to get your father's coin back for you," I said.

"Does Jimmy have it?" she asked.

"It looks that way," I told her, "and though I hate to say this, it looks as if your family may have been right about Jimmy. They probably had all the wrong reasons, but I'm beginning to think that he's not very nice."

"So am I," she agreed, "but what made you think of him? He did get a bad beating."

"That's the strange part," I said, "but right now, I feel like having some Dunkin' Donuts and coffee. I have a lot to do yet, so I'll tell you the whole story some other time. One thing I want you to do is keep quiet about the coin even if your parents come home before I can get back here. I think I'm going to get the coin, so you just wait for me. If, for some crazy reason, your father goes right to his coin folders and see's that one of them is missing, you act surprised. Can you do all that?"

"Sure," she answered, "but are you sure you'll get the coin?"

I couldn't blame her for doubting me, but I was almost certain this time and told her so. We walked to her front door. "There's another thing you have to do for me," I said, "and this is important. When you think Sherri's up, call her. Tell her that I'm going to pick her up around seven. Tell her to be in front of her house. You can tell her what you know, but please make sure she's there."

"She'll be there," Karen assured me. "She was really feeling bad for you last night."

The donut shop on Foothill Boulevard was open, so I parked in the lot. It was empty, and there weren't any customers in the shop. I wondered how they could keep open twenty-four hours a day. The guy inside was busy making sheets and sheets of donuts. Evidently, business picked up a lot once daylight hit. I hoped the guy cheered up, too, because he certainly didn't act happy to see me.

I had three donuts. Either they were smaller than I remembered, or I was hungrier than I imagined. They were sweet enough to remind me that I was going to have to get back to doing situps every morning. I ate fast because the guy was paying more attention to watching me than he was to watching his donut sheets. I guessed he'd been reading too many news stories about drug-crazed teens pulling holdups, but I couldn't imagine that I looked like one. I probably didn't, but the guy wasn't taking any chances.

It was partly cloudy when the sun made its first appearance of the day. I looked at my watch and saw that it was 6:20. If the sun came up the same time the next day, I wasn't going to be one of the people welcoming it. Once a year was enough. I climbed into my car and drove to Sherri's. I had time to spare, but I was hoping she'd be outside early. She was.

The dress she was wearing looked fine, but I liked her a lot more in jeans. Her mother probably liked dresses for school. She smiled over at me as she slid into her seat and closed the car door. "Karen told me everything," she said. "I would have never guessed it."

"It's not over yet," I said, starting my engine. "So far, all we have is a good reason to think that Jimmy might have the coin. We still have to get it and by the way, I got you out early because I figured you knew where Jimmy lives."

"I was wondering why you wanted me to come along," she said, and followed that with the directions to Jimmy's house.

"I didn't only want you along for directions," I said when she'd finished. "I figured you'd want to be around at the end of this, too."

"I do," she said, gently touching my arm. "I was just teasing you."

I parked across the street from Jimmy's house. I wanted to wait for him rather than barge into the house. "There's no sense in getting his grandmother upset," I told Sherri. "I'm sure she doesn't know a thing about this."

Jimmy's car was parked out in front of the house. He lived close to the high school, but Sherri assured me that he drove to school every day. So we waited. It wasn't long before he stepped out of the front door. He was wearing his sunglasses. I didn't know if he needed them anymore, but I figured he might if he decided to give me some trouble. I got out of my car as fast as I could, leaving Sherri to decide if she wanted to follow me or watch from the car.

Jimmy must have smelled trouble with the sight of me. He quickly decided that he wasn't driving to school and started running down the street. That move surprised me and gave him a little lead, but he was slow. If he thought he was running for his life, he didn't seem to care much about it. A block away, I tackled him. He went down as easy as a three-legged dog. "I didn't do anything," he cried into my ear.

"Who said you did?" I asked. "Sherri and I came to offer you a ride to school and instead of being happy to see us, you ran away."

Jimmy wasn't buying that. The look on his face told me so. "Just let me alone, will you?" he begged, just as Sherri stepped up alongside of us.

"No," I said angrily, "you're going to talk and maybe after that I'll decide not to do anything to the good parts of your face. Now let's get up and if you try to run again, you'll be limping after I catch you."

We stood up. For a fleeting moment, Jimmy considered his chances of running for it. His memory was good. "Okay," he said, "you talk all you want."

I grabbed him and pulled him toward me. "If you're smart, you'll talk, too," I warned him. "First, tell me when you decided to take the coin."

Jimmy surprised me. He gave up a lot faster than I thought he would. "As soon as I got my hands on it," he said. "I knew what it was worth, and I knew Karen's old man would be sick when he found out it was gone."

"Did you have to get beat up to make it all look good?" I asked.

Jimmy sneered. "That was all an accident," he answered. "I planned to say that I lost the coin on one of the rides, but those stupid bikers showed up. I mouthed off to them because I didn't like them. I didn't plan on the beating, but once I realized what they'd done to me, I threw the missing coin thing on them. They deserved it. Anyhow, I had to get something out of the beating."

"What about your money?" I asked.

Jimmy almost laughed. "I was just about broke that day of the fair," he said. "So I decided to make it seem like the coin had been taken along with my money. I thought it would seem more likely that the bikers would be after cash. They wouldn't have known anything about rare coins, and even if Karen's old man blamed me for losing the coin, she'd be able to tell him that I'd lost my money, too."

"It's too bad that you knew about rare coins," I said. "Now we're up to the big question. I'm hoping for you that you didn't sell that coin. If you did, I'm turning this whole thing over to the police."

"Forget the police," Jimmy said smugly. "You can have the lousy coin. It's been in the same place since last Wednesday."

Sherri and I followed Jimmy to his car. Just before he lifted out the front seat, he said, "I was really trying to think of some way to sell the coin back to Karen's old man. I don't like him at all."

The coin was under the seat just where Jimmy had dropped it. He picked it up and handed it to me. "Did you tell Karen about me?" he asked.

"Yes," I said, "I told her. Her father told her a long time ago, but we're all slow learners about some things. You're a little slow about taking other people's property."

"Can I go now?" Jimmy said, smirking at me.

I grabbed him by the neck and slammed him into his car. "Sure," I told him, "but just let this advice sink into your miserable little head. Stay away from Sherri and Karen. Don't even bother saying hello to them. If you do, I'm coming after you and I'm going to put a dent in you like the one your little act put into my trunk."

Jimmy thought better of telling me that he wasn't worried. He didn't answer, but he didn't have any questions. I left him trying to get his front seat back in place.

Fifteen minutes later, Sherri and I roared into Karen's driveway. She was waiting outside and ran over to the car. I handed her the coin. "Thanks," she said, staring at the coin. "I can't thank you enough and you, too, Sherri."

"I guess your parents didn't show up yet," I said.

"Any minute now," she answered.

"Then go put the coin back where it belongs," I told her. "We have to go. Sherri can call you later and tell you everything that happened."

"I will," Sherri said excitedly. "It was great, Karen, really great."

Karen ran off, and I raced off. Sherri and I were going to be late for school, and we didn't have a good excuse. Maybe we really did, but there was no way to use it. Besides, the people in the office wouldn't have believed us. Kids never do the kinds of things we'd been doing. Adults were sure of that. So we used the old flat tire line. It worked, even though they didn't believe it.

Before leaving Sherri, I asked her to meet me at lunchtime. We'd meet at the Taco Treat. Harry would be there. He always was.

14

I met Sherri on the way to Taco Treat. When we arrived, I saw that Harry hadn't failed me. He was already eating. He was sitting outside at his usual table. "I told you he'd be here," I said. "Talk to him while I get us some food. Do you want a supreme and a Coke?"

She wanted a regular taco and a root beer. When I got back to the table, she and Harry seemed to be getting along wonderfully. "I told you he eats here every day," I said.

Harry looked down at what was left of his second burrito. "It's these crazy egg rolls," he said. "This place serves the best egg rolls in town."

Sherri and I laughed. I knew she'd already told him the good news about the coin, so he surprised me when he said, "How'd you ever figure out it was Jimmy?"

"Don't play it modest," I said, surprising him. "You gave me the whole thing last night."

Harry smiled at Sherri. "I have to hear this myself," he said.

"You were telling me about your electronic chess pal," I explained. "You told me you had to send it out to be fixed. Do you remember why?"

"Sure," Harry said, grinning at the two of us, "it was making moves before the game started, and you decided that Jimmy was doing the same thing. I didn't make the connection before, but I'm glad you did."

"When are you getting your electronic game back?" Sherri asked.

"Not for weeks," Harry said sadly. "They sell it quickly and fix it slowly. You know how that works."

"I'm not great at chess, but I could give you a good game," Sherri suggested. "Would you like to play some night?"

"I'd like to try to play you," Harry said, smiling at her. "You may be too good for me."

I couldn't believe my ears. Sherri almost melted when the words rolled out of Harry's mouth. "I doubt that," she said, standing and smiling at Harry and me, "but you call me and we'll make a date and see. Terry will give you my number. I have to go now and try to find out what I missed in my first class this morning. I'll see you later, Terry."

"Sure," I said, wondering if I would really run into her again that day at school.

"If not, call me," she said, starting away from the table, "and Harry, please don't forget to call."

As she walked off, I got the clear impression that I had a lot more to learn about girls. When she was out of sight, I shook my head and grinned at Harry. "Nice going," I said, "and I thought I could trust you. I couldn't believe it when you came on with that stuff about her being too good to play you in chess. How'd you come up with that line?"

Harry gave me one of his big smiles. "Popped right out," he said. "Didn't even have to think about it. If I was in good shape like you, I probably would have been able to hold it in."

"Don't start on my weightlifting now," I said. "It's bad enough that I just wasted a whole weekend. I might have met some girl who cared about muscles at the mall."

"Don't look up fast," Harry said, lowering his voice. "Just glance across the street at the dark-haired beauty coming this way. Do you see her?"

"I see her," I said, though the sun was in my eyes.

"She's coming from the office," he said. "She lost her bracelet with her name and address on it. I don't know why anyone would want to take her bracelet, but I told her about you. I told her that you're probably the only private eye working in any high school in America today. How was that for a buildup? She was quite impressed."

"I want to get back to working out," I said, "so save the buildups."

"She's nice," Harry replied.

I squinted as the girl got closer. She was nice. "I'll think about it," I said. "First, introduce me. I'm not rushing into anything."

"I didn't think you would," Harry said, trying hard not to smile. "I told her you were pretty busy right now, but she wanted to meet you anyhow."

I squinted again. Close up, she looked better than Sherri. Maybe not better, but as good as Sherri. I could listen. The sun felt good. It was hot. It was going to be a nice, hot smoggy day.

ABOUT THE AUTHOR

Mel Cebulash has written numerous books for young readers, including *Ruth Marini of the Dodgers* and two companion books about a young female baseball player: "A women pitcher for the Los Angeles Dodgers? Well, somehow Cebulash makes it all seem possible." (*Booklist*)

Although he grew up in New Jersey, Mr. Cebulash now lives in Southern California. He has been an active member of the Mystery Writers of America for many years and recently served as regional vice-president of the organization.

Lerner Publications Company
241 First Avenue North, Minneapolis, Minnesota 55401

FIC
CEB   Cebulash, Mel

HOT LIKE THE SUN

	DATE DUE		

CEB   Cebulash, Mel

HOT LIKE   THE   SUN

ESEA-93